KU-473-809

JUDGE COLT PRESIDES

When one of the powerful Ducane family is hanged for murder in a border town, his father wipes out the place in revenge. Deputy Federal Marshal Fargo Reilly goes south to dispense justice and becomes involved in a gun-running conspiracy, and a plot to murder the president of Mexico. Reilly and his deputy Matt Crane fight to destroy the gang. But can Reilly also stop them from ransacking the nearby town of Perdition, where *Judge Colt Presides*?

Books by George J. Prescott
in the Linford Western Library:

RANGELAND DETECTIVE
SILVER SPURS AND LEAD
RUSTLER ROUNDUP
GUNS ON THE WAHOO
KILLING IN CARTUNA

WOLVERHAMPTON LIBRARIES			
SNU			
		3 0 NOV 2008	
478991			

GEORGE J. PRESCOTT

JUDGE COLT PRESIDES

Complete and Unabridged

LINFORD
Leicester

First published in Great Britain in 2007 by
Robert Hale Limited
London

First Linford Edition
published 2008
by arrangement with
Robert Hale Limited
London

The moral right of the author has been asserted

Copyright © 2007 by George J. Prescott
All rights reserved

British Library CIP Data

Prescott, George J.
    Judge Colt presides.—Large print ed.—
Linford western library
    1. Western stories
    2. Large type books
    I. Title
    823.9′2 [F]

    ISBN 978–1–84782–433–2

Published by
F. A. Thorpe (Publishing)
Anstey, Leicestershire

Set by Words & Graphics Ltd.
Anstey, Leicestershire
Printed and bound in Great Britain by
T. J. International Ltd., Padstow, Cornwall

This book is printed on acid-free paper

1

'You're dancin' with my gal, cow nurse!' The ugly words hung in the air, bringing the young cowhand to whom they were addressed around to face his accuser.

'Shucks, mister,' the boy began, 'there's plenty o' Miz Maudie's gals free to dance with and Ellie here, waal, she's kinda spoke for.'

'S'right, mister,' the slim, dark-haired girl, whose arm was entwined in that of the young cowboy, confirmed cheerfully.

'Any of the other gals'll be happy to help you spend your money, though,' she added hopefully.

'But I want you!' snarled the big hook-nosed stranger wearing a pair of Colts, stepping back and laying a practised hand on his pistol. 'Unless, o'course, you got any objection, cow

1

nurse,' he finished, with a sneer.

'I ain't wearin' a gun, mister . . . ' the boy began, raising his hands carefully away from his worn vest.

'Lucky me!' the other snarled, snatching out a pistol and driving a bullet into the youngster's chest.

Instantly, a dozen guns menaced the killer and the three evil-visaged Mexicans who had closed up around him. Having rapidly divested the group of their weapons, a hard-faced old-timer wearing the badge of town marshal, knelt by the boy and the tearful girl who was stroking desperately at his face as if to will the life back into him.

'How's Thad?' one of the group surrounding the killer demanded harshly.

'Cashed,' the old man confirmed, rising to his feet and approaching the boy's killer. 'And it was just plain murder!'

'Murder, hell!' the hook-nosed killer snarled. 'He was reachin' for a gun. Had a derringer under his vest.'

'Nope,' the old peace officer stated

simply, 'Young Thad was standin' up with his hands away from his sides. Never made a move for a gun, 'cause he hadn't got one.'

'I'm tellin' you, mister, he was reachin' for a gun,' the killer yelled, although what came out was three parts whine. 'He had a hide-out. You saw it, didn't you, Diego?' he went on, addressing the filthy Mexican at his side.

'*Sí, señor,*' the man confirmed with a sneer, 'he try to kill the *señor* here.'

'I hate to call a man a liar when he ain't carryin' a gun, but that's just about all you are, *hombre*!' the old man snapped. 'An' if'n I hear another lie from you, you damn greaser,' he went on, addressing the Mexican, 'you'll hang with your damned boss.'

'What d'you mean *hang*?' the killer demanded, voice rising shrilly, 'You can't hang me!'

'Why not?' the old man retorted harshly.

''Cause I'm Buck Ducane,' the

3

hook-nosed one snarled. 'An' if any-thing happens to me, my pa and my brothers'll wipe this one-horse pile of cow droppin's off the face of the earth.'

'Word says them Ducanes are bad *hombres*, Webb,' one of the younger cowhands pointed out mildly to the older man. 'Might be best to hold him for the US marshal.'

For a moment, Webb appeared to be thinking.

'That piece o' filth shot young Thad like I would a coyote,' he began softly. 'Then he turns coward and tries to hide behind his family. If this is the best the Ducanes can do, I figure we ain't got much to worry about. Jay,' he went on, turning to the nearest of the younger men, 'find the judge, tell him we got some court business for him. Then get a good rope and find this fella's pony.'

* * *

The chilly hour before dawn found the tough old cottonwood on the outskirts

4

of the little town of Dragon Wells, where Buck Ducane had made his final fatal mistake, bearing his body, hanging by a rope-broken neck.

Below the slowly swinging corpse, Marshal Webb Paul was addressing three sullen Mexicans.

'You can cut that down at sun-up,' the old man said caustically, 'an' don't forget to tell his pa he died like a coward, beggin' for his life,' he finished flatly.

'As for you boys,' Webb went on, 'I ever see you in town again, you hang. Now vamoose!'

Turning to go, the three Mexicans engaged in a low-voiced conversation.

'What do we do, Diego?' demanded Paco, who was small and nervous, but very quick with a knife.

'If we go back to El Diablo Blanco and tell him we let them kill that fool, we ain't gonna live so long.'

'You know what is in those wagons, Paco?' Diego asked irrelevantly.

'Sure,' the little man agreed, 'but what . . . ?'

'If we don't go back, what do you think the Old Man gonna do? He don't care about Buck, he got other sons and Buck weren't no use anyhow. But what is in those wagons! *Madre de Dios*, they're worth a fortune. More than a fortune!' the Mexican went on. 'And the gringos, they ain't gonna let us move them!' he finished.

★ ★ ★

'Dragon Wells, you say, Diego?' the old, white-haired giant asked almost mildly. Only the fists, clenching and unclenching at his sides told of the internal struggle, the desperate attempt to hold his autocratic and unbending mind somewhere near the right side of sanity.

'*Sí, sí, patron*,' anxiously confirmed the tallest of the three men who had been with the late and largely unlamented Buck Ducane.

'We couldn't get the wagons without the gringos getting suspicious, so we left them and the horses there.'

6

'You left . . . goddamn it, what do I pay you yeller bastards for?' the old man thundered. 'You left my horses and the wagons and the g — '

'Pa!' the voice was insistent and deep in timbre, although clearly feminine. 'Best you think before you open your mouth again!'

Coming forward into the light of the lamp which occupied a nearby table, the speaker was revealed as a young woman, dressed for ranch work in shirt and worn, faded Levis. Big-framed and powerful-looking, her body had been filled out by incessant work until it bulked as large as any of her brothers.

'After that marshal hung Buck and rode them outa town, don't seem to me there was much else they could do, Pa,' she went on reasonably.

'How long ago did you leave Dragon Wells, Diego?' she demanded, turning to face the terrified Mexican.

'Three days,' the man responded nervously. 'We nearly kill the horses getting here.'

'Three days,' the woman mused. 'Mebbe they ain't even got around to opening them wagons yet. Pa,' she offered.

'Mebbe,' the old man agreed, temper now back under control, 'but we can't take no chances.

'Vicente,' he snapped at the tall, scar-faced *vaquero* who leaned nonchalantly against the wall of the sprawling ranch-house's main room.

'Send Owen in here to me, then tell the men to saddle up. All of them. Grub for six days and all the cartridges they can carry. We're riding north.'

* * *

Dawn, some four mornings later, found Dragon Wells and its inhabitants still enjoying their rightful slumbers before the heat of the New Mexican summer turned even the thick-walled adobes into ovens.

Just a morning like any other morning. Except this one found a

8

group of masked, well-armed riders forming a loose cordon around the town. Here and there a man reined his restive pony, both horses and men impatient for dawn and the signal it would bring.

Old man Ducane had laid his plans carefully and his final instructions had been viciously explicit.

'I want that marshal alive!' he'd snarled, 'He's gonna pay for what he did to Bucky. Kill all the rest! Leave none of them alive.'

Webb Paul, unable to shake a lifetime of habit, rolled from his blankets with the first pink light in the sky and clapping on his battered Stetson, blearily pushed through the rear door of the jail.

Without warning, his arms were pinioned, before he was deftly tripped.

Face down, his hands and feet were swiftly tied, then he was jerked upright to find himself face to face with Rosa Ducane.

Dispassionately, the woman slashed a

hard hand across the old man's mouth.

'You hanged my brother,' she stated matter-of-factly, 'so now you're gonna watch what happens to anyone who crosses the Ducanes.'

'Bring him!' she snapped in Spanish to the men who had accompanied her and, without waiting to see her orders obeyed, she stepped off the narrow boardwalk, drew her Colt and sent three shots into the still morning air.

In almost an echo of the signal, a chorus of screams and shouts rose from the watching cordon, as, spurring their ponies, they drove mercilessly through the little town, shooting down anyone and everything in their path.

In the one-storey adobe saloon, the yells and shooting had brought its owner, Maudie Jones, instantly awake. Pausing only to wrap herself in a gaudy silk dressing-gown and snatch up the battered sawn-off shotgun which had lived next to her bed since Webb Paul had hanged Buck Ducane, she hurtled through the door and into the big bar-room, as the sound of shots split the air.

Just inside the still swinging batwing doors stood three masked riders, their pistols trailing smoke to the ceiling. Jud Pope, her bartender, lay huddled beside the big polished bar which had been his pride and joy, the back of his head blown off. Next to him was one of the girls, while the rest formed a screaming group against the rear wall.

Almost of its own volition, the shotgun in her hands jerked upwards and fired, unfortunately missing the three men and discharging its load into the nearby wall.

Fluidly, the nearest of the three turned, lifting his gun towards her and firing in one smooth motion. Brilliant lights mushroomed inside the lady saloon-keeper's head and she knew no more.

★   ★   ★

Maudie Jones awoke to the feel of smoke, acrid and burning, filling her lungs and a banging inside her skull as if it contained all the hammers of Hell working together.

Slowly, her vision cleared and she was able to make out the still forms of Jud Pope and the girl and, with that sight, realization dawned. The bastards had fired her saloon.

Painfully, the woman crawled across the hard-packed dirt floor until she reached the front wall.

Moving carefully, she inched her way along until she could peer around the lower edge of the door-frame. What she saw there sent her wriggling backwards, despite the smoke and imminent danger.

Hatless and erect upon a giant white stallion, Ducane directed his men for all the world like some Old Testament patriarch landed in a later time of the world.

Suddenly, the doors of the big barn facing the saloon were thrust back, revealing several high-sided, broad-tyred wagons, piled high with stacks of wooden boxes.

Spurring forward, the old man screamed, 'Git them goddamn wagons outa that place and then burn it! Burn the whole place! Everything! Burn it to the ground!

'Then, bring me that law-dog,' Ducane added, with a smile of cruel relish, as he drew a long bladed Bowie knife from its sheath at his side, 'and a coupla hot irons and a good rope.'

2

'While they . . . was finishing with Webb . . . Marshal Paul, I mean, I managed to sneak out of my place. I hid out until nightfall, then I stole me a horse and hightailed it for Mimbreño Station, that being the nearest place I figured I could get help. Never would have made it, 'cept I got found by some Mex sheepherders. They tended me and brought me on there and I got a stage to Tuscon.'

Maudie Jones came to a stumbling halt in her narrative and looked across the brilliantly polished desk at the lean, grey-haired man with the mild eyes who was seated there.

'And what exactly do you expect me to do, Miss Jones?' The voice, like the eyes, was mild and courteous. Somehow, the mildness goaded Maudie Jones's barely controlled anger to the surface.

'For Christ's sake,' she spat, 'you're the goddamn governor! If you can't do somethin' about them bastards, Mr Lane Clements, I'd like to know who in hell can?'

'Waal now, Miz Jones,' Clements began quietly, ignoring the lean cowboy who was the only other occupant of the big, comfortably furnished room, 'the problem we got here is one of what's called jurisdiction.

'Although them Ducane coyotes committed their crime in Arizona, their ranch is in Mexico,' he explained, 'and that means, legally, we can't touch them.'

'So you're just gonna let them get away with it!' the woman snapped. 'Goddamn it, Governor, there was a hundred people in that town, women and kids too, and those bastards just butchered them like . . . like . . . like they was cattle! You got to stop them!'

Before Clements could reply, the cowboy said gently. 'About them wagons, ma'am. Did the boxes have any marks on them? Think deep, ma'am, if you would,' he went on, as the woman opened her mouth to reply, 'it could be real important.'

Caught by surprise, Maudie Jones snapped her mouth shut on her response and looked warily at the governor, who said quickly, 'This is Mr Reilly, ma'am, an . . . associate of mine. You may consider any questions he asks as coming directly from me.'

'I didn't see no marks,' the woman began emphatically, after a few moments' thought, 'but I couldn't see them boxes real clear, though, just where the tarp had shifted at one end. They looked pretty solid, like they was made to take somethin' heavy, if that's any help.'

'Could be, ma'am,' Reilly offered reassuringly. 'What about the men themselves, especially their leader, old man Ducane?'

'They was mostly greasers and a coupla white men,' she said haltingly. 'Looked like they'd do any sort o' meanness and like it, just so long as

they was paid. But the old man . . . '
She paused.

'I heard them,' she went on, gazing
vaguely towards the big window behind
Clements's head, and it seemed to the
watching cowboy that something stirred
in her beyond the sight of those in the
room.

'I heard them,' she repeated, voice
dropping to a whisper, 'after they
hanged old Marshal Webb. They were
laughing and then one of them said
suddenly — I think it must have been
one of the greasers — *El Diablo
Blanco*. Then they all went quiet and
the old man hisself rode up and sat
looking at the marshal, just swinging
there . . . with . . . the blood runnin' off
him.' She shuddered.

'Did he say anything?' Reilly prompted.

'No . . . just looked and then . . . he
. . . smiled and . . . and I come away.'

For a long moment, all was silence.

'What else?' Reilly asked softly. The
woman shrugged substantial shoulders.

'Nothin' . . . much,' she whispered.

'Just sometimes . . . I dream about that time . . . and . . . when I do . . . I see him smiling at me.

'Mr Reilly,' she went on quietly, 'It was the sort of smile you'd see on the face of the Devil hisself while . . . while . . . he was torturing lost souls!'

* * *

'O' course, you ain't figuring on letting them get away with it, are you, Governor?' Reilly stated mildly.

Maudie Jones had gone, clearly disappointed in the forces of law and order then operating in Arizona Territory, and the two men had smoked in silence, a silence only broken by Reilly's soft-voiced question.

'No, I ain't, goddamn it,' Clements snapped. His voice hadn't risen, but there was a metallic timbre to that Reilly knew well and the cold eyes beneath the iron-grey brows were as hard as flint.

'That rats' nest needs cleaning out,'

Clements went on, 'and I'm sayin' the job needs doin' right! It'll take someone with brains and gun-speed — '

'Not to mention a fair slice o' luck,' Reilly interrupted, matter-of-factly, 'When you figure I should start, Lane?'

For a moment, the older man glared into the untroubled blue eyes of his companion, then his glance dropped.

'I just plain wouldn't feel right about orderin' you to go, Fargo,' Clements stated flatly, 'and I won't ask you . . . you know the sort ol' man Ducane is. If he catches you' — Clements paused — 'you'll be a long time lookin' for death afore it comes. And if the Mexican Government get their hands on you, well, I couldn't help you, either. No law down there, neither.'

'You mean I'm on my own.' Reilly smiled cynically. 'Well, that ain't nothin' unusual. An' you're wrong,' he went on, rising and sauntering towards the door.

'There's law courts down there. Only they all has Judge Colt presiding,' he finished, touching the worn butt of his right-hand pistol, as he took down his wide-brimmed Stetson.

'Where you figuring to start?' Clements asked, as the other paused with his hand on the door knob.

'Dragon Wells,' came the short answer. 'Them wagon tracks has got me sorta interested.'

★ ★ ★

'Whatever it was they was shippin', it was durn heavy, Pecos.' Reilly offered, as he carefully examined the wagon ruts leading away from the pile of ash and twisted metal which had once been Dragon Wells's only livery barn.

'Wide wheels, too,' he went on, measuring the tracks with his hand. The small, iron-hard paint mustang, ground hitched well clear of the tracks, nodded his ugly hammer head emphatically, as if in agreement.

'Glad you concur, son,' Reilly grinned, giving the off-key, two-note whistle which brought Pecos trotting to his side.

'Nothing more to see here, I guess,' Reilly offered, swinging aboard. Unconsciously hitching his battered gunbelt with its twin, worn-butted Colts, he reined the little mustang towards the trail out of town, before muttering, 'We got business south.'

★　★　★

Reilly had left Tuscon before dawn on the day following his meeting with the governor, completing the journey to Dragon Wells in easy stages, so as to keep his mount as fresh as possible. He well knew the iron strength and endurance in that stunted, muscular body and had often been forced to ask it for more than any man had a right to expect or any pony had to give. But Pecos had never failed him and so, cowboy-like, Reilly invariably took better care of the little mustang than he did of himself.

Topping the rise which the trail took as it left the little town, now just a collection of ashes left as a stark memorial to the Ducanes' displeasure, Reilly scanned the trail ahead and, finding the characteristically deep wheel ruts he was looking for, kneed Pecos gently forward into an easy lope.

'Guess this is as good a way as any to get where we want to go, ol' hoss,' Reilly muttered, but the look in his cold blue eyes boded little good for any Ducane who might cross his path.

* * *

'So what do you figure to do about this federal marshal the governor's sending, Pa?'

'Whyn't we just kill him, Pa?' the thin reedy voice went on, its owner a rat-faced individual dressed in an expensive suit of tailor-made range clothes.

'You ain't never had the sense of a pile o' horse dung, Owen,' his father snapped angrily, while Rosa and her three other brothers, the only other occupants of the big untidy, main room of the Ducane ranch-house, shared malicious smiles.

'If he's only sent one man, that means he must be very good,' the old man went on. 'Mebbe too good to monkey with.'

'How come you're so sure the governor sent this son of a bitch, Pa?' Rosa demanded.

'I got ways,' came the short answer and Rosa sullenly relapsed into silence. This wasn't the first time she had had an inkling of the breadth of her father's organization and, insanely quixotic though he might be in some matters, she knew a shrewd intelligence guided his business dealings.

Long ago, Rosa knew she needed to understand the full extent of his diverse holdings before she could realize her own dream of becoming head of a new and greater Ducane empire. Rosa, in her own special way, was well on her way to becoming madder than her father.

'I could take 'im, Pa,' rumbled the giant voice of Bull Ducane, eldest of the old man's children, breaking in on his sister's thoughts. 'I'll rip his goddamn head clean off!'

'If he lets you get close enough,' Rosa sneered.

'Mebbe we can arrange that,' Owen countered evilly.

★   ★   ★

On a sun-baked afternoon five days after leaving Dragon Wells, Reilly pulled his tired pony to a halt just below the breast of a gentle rise in the trail he had been following for the past two days, and which appeared to be the only pass through the wall of rock which separated the coast from the rugged country through which he had recently passed.

Before him lay the typical mixture of clapboard and adobe buildings which passed for a town on the Border, while Reilly could just make out the hazy blue of the Gulf of Mexico beyond.

Just off the trail leading to the dusty, rubbish-littered main street was a sign. With difficulty, Reilly made out the faded lettering. It was just one word: 'Perdition'.

'I sure bet it's all o' that, Pecos,' Reilly grunted cynically.

The wagon tracks he had been following had disappeared after crossing several weary miles of lava outcrop a couple of days after leaving Dragon Wells and rather than waste time finding them again, Reilly had located and followed a faint trail which he knew headed in the general direction of the Ducane ranch.

After a careful survey of the town, Reilly remained deep in thought for some moments, only to be aroused by Pecos, jerking on the reins. The little mustang smelled water, but, reluctantly, his master turned him back up the trail they had been following.

'We need us an ace in the hole afore they know we're here, Pecos,' he explained, kneeing the little pony into a distance-eating lope, 'and I'm saying we may need it bad.'

Reilly's 'ace in the hole' soon showed itself in the form of a faint track leading away from the main trail, into a tiny forest of stunted pines. Following it hopefully, Reilly eventually found himself looking into a small box canyon which contained a plentiful supply of the wiry bunch grass characteristic of the region, its good forage explained by a tiny stream which chattered through the rock on one side of the canyon, ending in a small pool well back from the entrance.

'Could have been made for us,' Reilly grunted, as he swung down and began unsaddling.

With Pecos rubbed down and picketed well away from the water, Reilly began his own preparations.

A brief examination of the end wall of the canyon revealed a number of holes in the crumbly rock. Selecting one with a good overhang, which would protect its contents from any rain, Reilly made a compact, oilskin-wrapped bundle of his old holstered Remington and a hundred cartridges, which would fit all of his pistols. Placed in the hole and packed with stones and dust, its presence was undetectable from the outside.

'Sure wish I had a coupla airtights,' Reilly muttered doubtfully, 'and a spare Winchester'd be a sight more'n handy.

'If'n we has to run,' he went on, turning away from his cache to begin preparations for his own meagre supper, 'we might be more in need o' grub and water than just about anything else.'

3

'This deal is looking worse all the time,' Reilly offered as he drew his pony to a halt on the rise from which he had examined Perdition the previous day.

'Ain't but one way in or out o' that flea pit, less'n you want to swim,' he went on, 'and then it's about a hundred miles to land in any direction. An' that trail looks like the only way down from the hills as well!'

After a fireless night spent in the little canyon, dawn had found Reilly riding a wide circle through the hills and then cautiously across the flat plain that led down to miles of sandy beach and towering cliffs which protected the town from the sea. He had ridden a full circle around Ducane's town in an attempt to find another trail in. His search had proved fruitless and early afternoon of the second day had found him literally back where he started.

'Gw'an, you ol' reprobate,' Reilly went on, giving Pecos a thump with his spurless heels which provoked a vicious snap from the big yellow teeth, 'I guess a bag of oats and a spell o' loafin' ain't gonna do you one bit of harm.'

Arriving on the main street of the dirty little town, however, Reilly found himself a witness to impending tragedy.

Two men were holding a young Apache, little more than a boy, while Owen Ducane stood flicking a quirt against his boot.

'Hold that l'il bastard — ' Ducane began, when a hard, cold voice broke in.

'I ain't sure what goddam dog's work's comin' off here,' Reilly snapped, coming to stand where all three men would be conveniently under his guns, 'but it sure as hell stops now.'

'This is Ducane business,' the bigger of the two men retorted, pushing the Indian boy so that he fell into the dust, and beginning to step away from his partner.

'Stand still, if you wanna live to see another sunrise,' Reilly ordered and all three men froze because, in a flickering blur of motion, Reilly's Colts were in his hands and menacing the group.

'Now we're all friendly,' the man with the drop grated. 'Shuck your belts. Be real careful,' he snapped, both guns lifting, 'I got a nervous disposition and these guns go off real easy when I'm using 'em for snake killin'.'

'You're makin' a big mistake, mister,' Ducane sneered, as he complied. 'This is a Ducane town and you better remember that.'

'Pick up them guns,' Reilly snapped at the youngster, in guttural Apache, 'and don't get between me and the white-eye.'

'Your name Ducane, is it, mister?' Reilly asked mildly as the youth swiftly obeyed. Receiving a malicious grin of confirmation, he went on dispassionately, 'Waal, I sure hope you ain't the pick o' the litter, 'cause if you are, the rest must be a real prize set o' yeller dogs.'

Holstering his right-hand Colt, Reilly bent swiftly, snatched up Ducane's quirt and in a single, lightning swift movement, slashed the rat-faced one across the cheek.

Ducane screamed and staggered backwards, clutching his lacerated face, as in a continuation of his previous movement, Reilly hurled the lead weighted quirt into the face of the nearest man, before sending his right hand across to fan the hammer of his Colt in a flickering burst of speed.

Struck by the quirt, the first Ducane rider staggered backwards, to land face down in the street as succesive shots from Reilly's pistol tore off his hat, both boot heels and two of the fancy buttons from his vest. The other Ducane man had barely time to step towards his companion before he found himself menaced by Reilly's second Colt.

'Up on the Panhandle, which is the part of the great and sovereign state of Texas where I come from,' Reilly explained conversationally, 'we like to ear crop our vermin.'

His Colt cracked three times, the shots sounding almost as one, his bullets neatly tearing off the left earlobe of each of the Ducane riders and their boss.

'Just so's we can be sure and recognize them again,' he finished mildly, holstering his Colt in one deft movement.

'Oh, you'll recognize us again, mister,' the taller of the two gunmen snarled, feeling gingerly at his ear.

'We'll be the ones holding the rope you'll be dancin' on the end of.'

'There's others can use a rope, mister,' Reilly responded softly. 'Mebbe you an' your boss got too much in the habit of it lately. Take a piece of friendly advice: leave that yeller dog at the ranch house, get your stuff and ride on, 'cause the next bullet you catch from me won't be headin' for your ear.'

Reilly had watched the three injured Ducane men until the group became just a blur against the sun of late afternoon, when he felt a diffident tug on his shirt sleeve.

It was the young Apache and Reilly smiled as he said in the deep-chested Mimbreños dialect. 'Your father's lodge would be proud of you today.'

Violently, the boy shook his head, pointing up the street in the direction taken by the Ducane riders and then drawing a finger savagely across his throat in the murderous, age-old gesture of defiance and threat.

'Should have killed them, you reckon?' Reilly mused in English and the boy answered with a single savage nod.

'You could be right,' he admitted, before asking gently. 'What's your name, son?'

'He can't talk, mister,' a cracked old voice said, almost in his ear and Reilly jumped back, turning and flashing a hand to his pistol in one lightning movement.

'You got quiet feet, partner,' Reilly offered, holstering his weapon and inspecting the old man who had caused his actions and was now standing with a pair of callused hands level with his shoulders.

Reilly's glance flicked momentarily over those hands, noting the significance of the size and position of the calluses, then he was looking into a pair of bleary eyes and the old man was repeating, 'He can't talk, mister, on account of Owen Ducane cut out his tongue a year or two back.'

'What in hell did he do that for!' Reilly demanded, shocked out of his usual indifferent composure.

'Tried to make the boy lick his boots for a bet and when young Mangas here spat in his face, he had two of them sons of bitches hold him, while he done the thing hisself.'

'Didn't nobody do anything?' Reilly wondered aloud.

'Huh.' The old man spat, while the young Apache's glance flicked between the two, following their conversation. 'Anybody who'da been willin' to try was either killed or run out long ago.

'It's like Owen said,' the old man

finished, 'this is a Ducane town!'

'But it doesn't have to be,' a youngish woman asserted as she limped up to the group.

'I'm Lauren Wex, *alcalde* of Perdition, on account of nobody else wantin' the job,' she went on, extending a slim, worn hand, 'and I'd like to thank you for saving my good friend Mangas here,' she finished, gently ruffling the boy's coarse black hair, to his infinite embarrassment. Reilly tendered his own name, only remembering to diffidently drag his hat off at the last moment.

'Don't you listen to Miz Lauren,' the old man snapped, a trace of fire in the bleary eyes. 'If'n I was you, Mr Reilly, I'd fork that l'il paint and get the hell away from this hell-hole just as fast as you can!'

'First of all,' Reilly began, 'you might find Fargo comes easier than all that 'misterin' ', and secondly, I can't leave, 'cause I come here just exactly to land the town marshal's job.'

'What?' the old man exploded,

although the woman's eyes were calculating. 'You must be loco!'

'It ain't etti-quet to insult someone afore you've been introduced, formal like,' Reilly politely informed the fuming old man, noting with satisfaction the fierce, angry light in the faded green eyes that had now replaced the bleariness.

'Why I'll be teetotally goddamned if'n I'm gonna — '

'His name is Crane, Mr Reilly,' Lauren Wex interposed quickly. 'The children all call him Pop, but I think you'll find his given name is Matthew. I'll just get your badge,' she finished, making off in a breathless bustle.

'Bring back a coupla extra for my deputies,' Reilly called after her, ''cause I'm sure gonna need some high quality help.'

'Where you aimin' to get that?' Crane demanded suspiciously.

'I figure I'm lookin' at it,' Reilly returned mildly, carefully ignoring his new deputy's scowl.

'You must be plumb loco,' Crane said again, lowering his hand at the conclusion of his swearing-in as a deputy marshal of the small and seedy border hellhole known as Perdition.

'Well, that's mebbe so,' Reilly admitted, reaching absently into a pocket. Locating the object of his search, he placed a battered nickel-plated badge, bearing the words, 'Federal Marshal Territory of Arizona', on the spur-scarred and cigarette-burn-decorated desk at which he was sitting. Leaning back in the squeaky swivel chair he was occupying, he briefly explained the events that had led up to his journey to Perdition.

Speech seemed to have failed Crane as he glared down at the badge, but it came back with a rush as the glare was turned on his respected superior officer.

'Federal marshal!' he exclaimed. 'And the governor really, finally, got off his backside and sent you?' Crane went on, tone larded with disbelief.

'Keep your voice down, you ol' goat.' Reilly prodded. 'Ain't no use to let the whole place know.'

'You're sure as hell right about that!' Crane rasped, this time keeping his voice low. 'What d'you figure ol' Sirus Ducane's gonna do when he finds there's a federal marshal in town?'

'Throw me a welcome party?' Reilly suggested, innocently.

'It'll be a sure enough party,' Crane exploded, 'a necktie party, with you as the main attraction.'

'Well then, I guess we better see if'n we can't set a l'il crimp in his game,' Reilly said.

'Now, leave us play another l'il game,' he went on, ignoring his furious deputy, 'it's called 'Guess what the nasty ol' bandit's gonna do so's we can out-fox him'. You can go first, Deputy Crane.'

All trace of ill-temper instantly vanished from the other's face, to be replaced by a look of brooding thought. The old man's eyes were hard and level when he finally turned them in Reilly's direction.

'First thing that's plain is he can't just leave you. You've taken cards and he's got to call or fold.

'If he's got any sense, the first thing he'll do is offer you a job,' Crane went on shrewdly, 'but I been here goin' on ten year and I ain't never seen Sirus do anything that made sense yet!

'So he'll have to make an example of you,' Crane finished. 'He needs this town quiet and under his thumb, seemingly, and he can't allow you to stir things up.'

'Which is sure 'nough about the way I figure it,' Reilly confirmed, 'so here's what we're gonna do . . . '

* * *

'You figure the boy'll be all right?' Reilly demanded.

'Sure,' Crane confirmed, 'as long as he can keep his eyes off that Colt and holster you give him.'

39

'Hell.' Reilly shrugged. 'He's a good kid, got sand to burn and he's due to be a better man. Besides, man needs the right tools for the job. Like that Winchester carbine he was carrying,' Reilly finished with a wide grin.

'Well, the damn thing weren't no use to me, just rustin' away. Saved me the trouble o' cleanin' it!' Crane bridled instantly.

'Sure, the climate around here bein' so damp and all,' Reilly agreed easily.

'Oh, and by the way, Matt,' Reilly went on conversationally, 'I ain't paying no deputy who ain't carryin' somethin' on his hip. Liable to be trouble around here soon, so you best start in to wearin' your Colts again. And it mightn't be a bad idea to put in some practice.'

4

For a moment, the faded green eyes glared across the desk at Reilly, but just as suddenly, Crane's glance clouded and his shoulders slumped.

'You got the wrong man, Marshal,' he stated, almost formally, gaze dropping. 'Best I just sweep out the jail for you and watch any prisoners.

'Anyhow,' Crane finished, 'I don' know nothin' about guns.'

'Show me your hands,' Reilly asked gently, and when Crane had complied, Reilly stretched out his own to lie next to those of the older man.

'Matt, you're a sure enough liar,' Reilly said flatly, indicating the callused ridges on thumb and forefinger, which matched those on his own hand.

'Ain't but one way a man raises calluses like that and that's from handlin' a gun, and doing it regular.

'Oh, I'm admittin' you mebbe ain't held a pistol since you hit this place,' Reilly went on, before the other could speak, 'but before that you did and often. Fact is, I heard tell of a Matt Crane, quite some years ago now,' Reilly related, watching the other narrowly. 'Made hisself a rep marshalling up in them Kansas cow towns, around Wichita and Abilene. There was some who said he could've shaded ol' Wild Bill hisself.'

'Hickock had magic hands,' the older man stated authoritatively, and the eyes he raised to Reilly were hard and clear. 'I . . . Crane weren't that good, though I ain't sayin' that a man mightn't have had trouble livin' on the difference between 'em.'

'Sounds just like the sort of man I'm needin',' Reilly decided.

'That Matt Crane is dead,' the old man stated emphatically, dropping his glance once again. 'He was dead and buried ten year ago and he ain't comin' back. I'll go get us a coffee pot and fixings,' he finished quickly and was gone before Reilly had the chance of another word.

'Mebbe he ain't dead,' the man from Tucson offered at the unresponsive door. 'Could be he's only sleepin' and just needs wakin' up.'

* * *

Crane was back well before sundown and with the new pot producing the first essential of any office, law or otherwise, Reilly pointed his deputy into an adjacent chair, after the old man had supplied both with mugs of the strong, black brew.

'I'm needin' answers, Matt,' he began simply, ignoring the anxiety plain on the other's face.

'Just what is the set up with old man Ducane and this town?'

'Ain't sure,' the old man admitted, tension easing out of him as he scrunched down in the comfortless chair. 'When I rode in here, 'bout ten year ago,' Crane went on, 'this was just a normal, sleepy, l'il border town. Oh sure, the boys from Ducane's spread spent their coin here, but the cattle business being what it was — '

'And still is — ' Reilly interrupted.

'And still is.' Crane nodded in agreement. 'The ol' man was having trouble keepin' his head above water.'

'That weren't no different from how things were and still are all over. Worse here, even, mebbe,' Reilly mused, ''cause there ain't no chance of any company runnin' a rail spur this far south.'

'Am I tellin' this or you?' Crane demanded. 'Not that I ain't sayin' you've called it about right.

'Anyhow,' Crane went on reflectively, 'that was how it stood. Ducane had cows, an awful lot of 'em, but mostly scrub stock, and folks back East expect their beef a mite tenderer than what you'd cut off'n one o' them hard-assed beeves.'

'So he was stuck with cows he

couldn't sell?' Reilly enquired.

'Right,' Crane agreed, with a terse nod. 'Then, seemed like overnight, he starts hiring men. He fires every single one of the old crew and starts takin' on the worst collection of border scum I ever seen.

'Funny thing is, though,' Crane continued, 'things around here didn't change much. There weren't never much trouble with his old crew, just a few windows shot out and damages were allus paid for. But the new men never give any sort o' trouble at all. And that was funny considerin' the sort of *hombres* they was.'

'Mebbe you was wrong about Ducane's new men,' Reilly asked innocently. 'Could be he'd took to hirin' choirboys?'

'Listen, you smart-ass kid,' Crane snapped, his glare hard and clear again. 'I've got so I can smell a *pistolero* in my goddamn sleep and you can take it from me, ol' Sirus has got the pick o' the bunch. Culled 'em special, too.'

'If you don't have no trouble with his

riders, what in hell's the matter with this town?' Reilly demanded.

'It ain't a town any more, is what's the trouble,' Crane retorted. 'It's just a place for Ducane men to spend their money.

'Lately it's changed, got worse. There's a lot of new hardcases come through, as well as the usual crew, and there's been a lot of killin'. Some townsfolk, too. Everybody's scared to death.'

'I want you to do somethin' for me, Matt,' Reilly said softly, as he rose, stretched and reached for his hat.

'Make a coupla signs,' he went on, in answer to the old man's enquiring look. 'Good big ones, stick 'em one at each end of town, where anyone comin' in can see 'em plain.'

'Sure,' Crane replied, 'easy enough done. What should I make 'em read?'

'Oh somethin' like, *No guns in town limits, by order: The Marshal of Perdition.*'

★   ★   ★

'It ain't exactly that business is bad,' Henry Vance, owner and operator of Perdition's only store explained.

'Ducane and his men spend their money here, got nowhere else to go, I guess,' he went on, confirming Crane's assessment, 'but it's like livin' on a powder keg, what with the killin's an' all. Nobody knows who's gonna be next.

'I'd leave, if I could,' the little man admitted, 'especially since my gal is gettin' to an age where she'd catch a man's eye.'

'Matt never said nothin' about women,' Reilly offered.

'Ain't a woman safe in this town,' Vance said darkly. 'Once Ducane's men ride in, I keep my wife and gal inside. They treat the Mexican girls and their men like dirt . . . or worse,' the little man finished.

'How many guns are there in town?' Reilly asked absently, 'and how many men who can use them?'

'Most of us can shoot, rifle or

shotgun, and I guess everyone's got some sort of weapon. I carry a fair stock out back as well,' Vance replied.

'Cartridges?' Reilly demanded.

'Every make and kind,'Vance acknowledged. 'Big stock, too, on account of Ducane's men needin' so many.'

'Better'n better,' Reilly answered, reaching for his battered Stetson and rising to leave. Pausing in the doorway, he turned, hat still in hand. 'This is your town,' he said, quietly. 'Will you and your friends fight to keep it? So you and your womenfolk and kids can live decent?'

'Hell, yes,' the little storekeeper snapped.

'All I needed to know,' Reilly returned, settling his worn headgear.

'Hold on, Marshal,' Vance interrupted. 'Having guns and cartridges is all very well, but you got to have men to use them. I doubt if there's a man in town who's ever even heard a shot fired in anger, let alone killed a man.'

'Killin' a man ain't a thing to be proud of,' Reilly growled and Vance was shocked at the depth of bitterness in the suddenly cold voice.

'Marshal . . . I . . . I never . . . I mean . . . ' Vance began breathlessly, before Reilly took pity on him.

'I figure the fact that you ain't never killed a man would be something more to be proud of,' Reilly said, and, once again, his voice was soft. 'Also, figure this: it's only the side I'm on that makes me different from Ducane's paid killers.

'Just a matter o' circumstances is all it needs,' he finished, 'as the man said who found hisself in the middle of a stampede without his pony.'

For a long moment after his visitor had gone, Henry Vance gazed at the dusty opening through which Reilly had departed. Then he grinned and shook his head.

'No, it don't!' he told himself emphatically, beginning to count bolts of cloth with more hope in his heart than had been there for many a day.

★ ★ ★

The sun was tilting under the horizon when Lauren Wex, sitting on the porch of the little house she occupied, almost outside Perdition's boundaries, found herself the recipient of a visit from her new town marshal.

'This town is needin a l'il backbone, Miz Wex,' Reilly began, without preamble, 'and I'm sayin it needs it right soon.'

Briefly, he explained what he had done so far.

'So what happens now?' Lauren Wex demanded.

'Well, I figure that Ducane is gonna try some sort of grandstand play, to make me look bad and put you and your folks back in their places. Especially you,' Reilly went on with a grin, 'on account o' you bein' the one who did the hirin'.'

'I'd like to kill them all,' came the low-voiced retort and Reilly, inured though his life had made him, was shocked by the violence in the tone.

'I could see how you might feel that

way, Miz Wex . . . ' he began diffidently.

'You see nothing, nothing, d'you understand?' the woman snarled, face twisting.

'They took . . . they took . . . ' With a titanic effort, the woman regained her self-control and when she next spoke, barely a trace of the violence remained.

'What must we do, Mr Reilly?' she demanded.

'Well, first, I want you to call a town meetin' tonight,' the man from Tucson began thoughtfully. 'Then I can tell everybody what I think's gonna happen and you folks can decide what you want to do. See, if'n it comes to it, I can ride on and me'n Pecos'll take our chances against that Ducane scum on the trail.'

'Would you get away if you did that?' the woman asked.

'We'd need a fair slice of luck,' Reilly admitted. 'However it come out, we'd sure take a few of them with us.'

Looking at the firm, grim line of the mouth and the low-tied guns, from

51

where the man's long, nervous fingers seemed never to be far, Lauren Wex found herself inclined to agree. Another one of her father's breed. Worse luck for him, she decided fretfully.

★   ★   ★

Full darkness had enveloped the street as Reilly left the marshal's office and began the short walk to Perdition's only cantina where Lauren Wex had suggested the town meeting should take place.

The building itself was well lit but, by contrast, the surrounding area was full of shadows and, intent upon the job before him, Reilly's instincts were slow.

He had just drawn level with entrance to one of the innumerable alleys which led away from the main street into the Mexican quarter of town, when two men appeared there.

Reilly's hands dropped to his guns, only to slow as he saw neither man appeared to be armed. His relaxation lasted only a moment, as a boot scuffed behind him.

Cat-quick, he turned, hands driving for his Colts, only to be struck on the side of the head by the glancing blow of a gun butt. Driven to his knees, he never felt the second blow, which tipped him over the edge and into oblivion.

In another of the alleys, a wide-eyed young Mexican boy had seen the whole incident and, swiftly identifying the marshal as a shaft of errant moonlight crossed his face, he turned and ran for a certain crumbling adobe on the outskirts of town. Reaching his destination minutes later, he hammered on the door.

'Señor Pop, Señor Pop,' he screamed. '*Señor*. In the cantina! The Marshal, he is in trouble.'

In the adobe, Matt Crane stirred, trying to throw off the whisky haze that enveloped him.

'Wha . . . whassermarrer, Miguel?' he began, recognizing the boy's voice.

'Señor Reilly. Señor Bull Ducane and four of his men. They are taking him to the saloon. Señor Pop, I think maybe they kill him, if he no get help.'

Desperately, Crane scrubbed shaking hands across his face.

'That boy don't deserve to die like a dog,' he blubbered. 'But what can I do, what can I do . . . ?'

5

Business in Perdition's small cantina was brisk that evening, as almost every adult male in town had turned up to hear what Fargo Reilly had to say.

'Of course, the *señor* marshal has no chance,' Pedro Gonzalez informed his listening friends.

'But suppose . . . ' began Amerigo Brazos, owner of the cantina, 'suppose such a thing were . . . ?'

Suddenly, the swing doors of the little building were smashed back against the spotlessly white adobe walls.

But the protest which sprang to its owner's lips, died away to nothing as two of Ducane's riders, both missing an earlobe, pushed roughly, through the entrance and hurled the limp body of their new town marshal across the crowded room to land against the rough planks of the bar.

Barely conscious, Reilly fought against a rising wave of nausea. Being wise in the ways of bar-room brawls, he made no attempt to rise, waiting instead for the slow clearing of his head to be accomplished.

Suddenly, he found his shirt front grabbed and he was lifted up to be slammed back against the bar. The hands left his shirt front and, through the fog in his head, he heard a deep, growling voice, coming from the centre of the bar-room.

'This piece o' scum beat up my brother and two of my pa's men,' it began. 'Now, we're gonna beat him to death and ride what's left outa town on a rail. Then we're comin' back and we're gonna hold another e-lection. And the scum in this town had better vote right or — '

'Don't sound very democratic to me,' a cold voice interrupted from the bar.

Reilly was standing with both elbows propped on the rough wood counter, as if to support himself. Carefully, he shifted his weight to one leg, waiting. He had one chance and that, to be honest, was pretty flimsy. The big man standing in the middle of the bar-room turned slowly in his direction.

'Sic 'im, Bull,' one of the Ducane men snapped unnecessarily.

'See the trouble with you, Mr Ducane,' Reilly went on evenly, 'is that, 'cause you come from a family of yeller dogs, like I told your brother, you expect everyone else to behave the same way.'

With a roar worthy of his namesake, Ducane leapt towards his tormentor. But Reilly wasn't there and, as the giant smashed into the bar where Reilly had been an instant before, the man from Tuscon stepped back in, driving a savage elbow into the man's kidneys and spiking his high-heeled boot into the side of Ducane's knee, eliciting a scream of agony and driving the big man to his knees.

Without hesitation, Reilly grabbed the giant's hair and jerked back his head, hammering a bunched fist into Ducane's Adam's apple.

The big man gagged, trying to jerk his head away and Reilly drove his merciless fist into the throat a second time, before the first of the Ducane riders smashed an uneducated fist into the side of his head.

Staggering back, Reilly was forced to release his victim, but not before, with a desperately lucky kick, he had smashed the toe of his boot up under Ducane's chin.

Desperately, he fought back against the Ducane men, but in his battered state, four opponents were far too many. A bottle finally descended on to his head, knocking him to his knees and, through the mist that had never quite cleared, he heard one of the three remaining Ducane men sneering, 'He fights good, but it ain't gonna save him. Wake Bull up and then get a rope — '

'You better bring a-plenty,' a hard, level, old voice interrupted from the doorway, ''cause if'n one o' you yeller sons of bitches touches him again, you'll be ridin' to hell so fast your short hairs'll burn.

'You're good there, Billy,' the cold voice snapped suddenly, and the chill in it had turned to ice. 'Just . . . right . . . there.'

Reilly forced his eyes open to see Matt Crane, in the doorway of the cantina. But this wasn't the old drunk everyone bought liquor for. This was a cold-faced, slit-eyed demon, balanced lightly on the balls of his feet, with two long-barrelled pistols in his hands, which looked as if they'd been grown there.

'Amerigo,' this apparition snapped, 'get the marshal on his feet and give him his guns.' But somehow the old man's attention must have wavered and the young man known as 'Billy the Kid', after the homicidal maniac who was his hero, saw his chance and sent a hand driving for his Colt.

Crane's left-hand gun barked once, the bullet tearing into the would-be killer's chest, followed almost instantly by the crash of the old man's second weapon, which drove a bullet into the forehead of the gunman standing to the kid's right, killing him before his weapon had cleared leather.

Without hesitation, Crane dropped his left-hand pistol and slapped his hand across to cock the hammer of his remaining weapon. But even before Crane's second weapon had hit the floor, Reilly was moving.

Jerking himself to his knees, he snatched the pistol from the belt of the Ducane rider standing in front of him. Unable to prevent himself from falling, Reilly jerked sideways, slamming two shots into the chest of the grinning tough who was even then lining his weapon on a helpless Matt Crane.

His victim lurched sideways and Reilly smiled up into the terrified face of the only Ducane rider left standing.

'Lucky for you we're needin' an undertaker,' he muttered, before fainting clean away.

Reilly came round to the sound of arguing. At least, one voice was arguing while the other expressed itself in meaningful grunts.

'A bucket o' water's the best cure for that sort of thing,' Crane's voice was insisting.

Forcing his eyes open past the imminent fog of nausea which threatened to envelop him, Reilly observed his elderly deputy, water bucket in hand, preparing to carry out his patent cure.

'Keep that goddamn ol' fool away from me,' Reilly growled, sliding upright on the comfortless bunk and glaring at his assistants.

'Where's Bull an' the other feller?' he demanded, trying desperately to get control of the Apache war party that was hammering around the inside of his head.

'Waal,' Crane began, elbowing his way past Mangas, who had been intent upon preventing any application of the old man's cure-all. 'We left Billy and Rafe an' the one you got with a lucky shot in the livery barn, on account of them not turnin' into any nosegays. Got Bull and Julio in the cell,' the old man explained.

'Together?' Reilly demanded.

'No!' the old man snapped. 'An' I took their guns too! Was that all right or should I give 'em back?'

'Naw,' Reilly grinned. 'You done all right for someone who don't know nothin' about guns.'

Before the fuming old gunman could begin to formulate a reply, Reilly had slipped from the couch and beckoned to the young Apache.

'What of the horses, brother?' he demanded, slipping into the easy, colloquial Mimbreños.

'All safe, father,' the young man signed respectfully, although his grin threatened his ears.

'Grass, water, or did you forget those, child?' Reilly went on, straight-faced.

'All is as it should be,' the hands almost snapped. 'Grass and water for four, mebbe five days,' although the smile on the younger man's face was pitying.

'Good,' Reilly grunted, sliding gratefully into a chair and accepting the inevitable mug of strong black brew from Crane.

'Pick out the best o' them ponies, Mangas, and he's yours,' Reilly went on easily, apparently ignoring the light that leapt into the boy's eyes. 'When we take the war trail, you're gonna need him. Meanwhile, get yourself a good feed and some sleep,' he finished, passing the boy some coins.

'Waal,' Crane began, 'you sure made a convert outa young Mangas. Boy thinks you're his favourite uncle and the Great Spirit all rolled into one.'

'You saved my neck back there, Matt,' Reilly stated flatly. 'Killed two Ducane men, too. Ducane ain't gonna be too pleased with you.'

'Damn right,' the old man said and

the red killing light flared briefly behind his eyes as he went on loudly, 'an' if'n you hadn't woke up pretty soon I was aimin' to have me a l'il private neck-tie party, with ol' Bull for the main attraction.'

'You ain't got the nerve, Crane,' came a deep, sneering voice from the cell block, although there was enough uncertainty in its tone to make Reilly grin.

The old man was on his feet in one cat-like move, a pistol miraculously in his hand as he moved up to the bars. Ducane cowered back before the venom in the agate hard eyes, although his mocking grin returned as Crane said softly, 'You really better hope none of your family makes me prove how wrong you are, bully boy.'

Noticing the bucket of filthy water he had used earlier to swab the floor of the jail, Crane remarked, 'You look hot, Bull,' holstering his pistol before lifting the bucket and jerking its contents over the big man. 'Laugh that off, you fat-gutted son of a bitch.'

'You finished?' Reilly demanded scathingly. 'And don't you know ill-treatin' prisoners is a federal offence?'

'Only if'n they're human,' Crane replied, with perfect equanimity, listening contentedly to the storm of abuse coming from the cells. 'An' I'm saying Bull sure don't qualify on that count.

'Just what are you aimin' to do with them two rattlers, Fargo?' Crane went on, 'Keep 'em 'till they die of old age?'

'Nope,' Reilly said loudly. 'There's a federal judge and a coupla marshals following me down. Soon as the judge gets here we'll have us a trial an' hang both o' them. Howsomever, that ain't what I'm concerned about now,' Reilly went on, noticing the cessation of abuse from the cells which had now been replaced by agitated, low-voiced muttering. 'What's botherin' me,' the man from Tuscon explained vehemently, 'is how you can shoot two *hombres* neat as I've ever seen it done, but then nearly get yourself killed 'cause you can't cock

65

your piece a second time. Is there mebbe something you oughta be tellin' me, Mr Crane?'

For a long moment, the old gunman glared across the table, but when he spoke his voice was mild, almost gentle.

'You treated me real decent, Fargo,' he began, 'but I ain't gonna be no good to you!' When Reilly made no comment, the old man said simply, 'I got arthritis in both my thumbs. I can hold a gun and I can still pull a trigger, but I can't use a thumb to cock the hammer. It has been comin' on gradual for years,' Crane added. 'An' when I nearly got a young fella killed who was deputyin' for me up on the Kansas border, I decided it was time I quit.'

'How come you ended up here?' Reilly enquired.

'Just happened,' Crane explained softly, 'This was where my money run out and I sold my horse and saddle. Bin here ever since.'

'Didn't sell your guns, though,' Reilly mused gently.

'Don't go readin' nothin' into that,' Crane snapped. 'They was just too old and beat up to fetch nothin'.'

'Let me see one o' them relics,' Reilly demanded.

The weapon Crane passed over was a Remington Army model, .44 in calibre. Originally a cap and ball revolver, it had been neatly converted to take metal cartridges and was clean and oiled, with a smooth hammer spur and barely perceptible trigger pull.

Reilly twirled the old gun on a muscular forefinger, liking the balance and smooth feel.

'That's a good weapon, Matt,' he began, tendering the old pistol butt first and reaching for his hat as he rose to his feet. 'Let's see if mebbe we can't figure somethin'.'

'You're a damn fool,' the old man snapped, clapping on his battered Stetson and instinctively settling the worn gunbelt, 'Whyn't you get some good help, 'stead of a rummy like me and that damn kid?'

'Dunno.' Reilly shrugged carelessly. 'Allus figured when my time come, I'd sooner die amongst friends.'

'You may just get your wish!' came the caustic response.

6

Behind the jail was a cleared area, where a former occupant of the office had marked out a makeshift shooting range.

'All right,' Reilly began, having set up an old door some twenty feet away, chalking a man-sized shape on it. 'Let's see what you can do.'

In answer, the old man's hand dipped in a sight-defying blur and suddenly there was a long-barrelled pistol in it, pointing down the range. The hammer of the single-action revolver was, however, still uncocked.

'You're still pretty fast,' Reilly complimented.

'Sure,' the old man admitted, 'but it ain't no use, 'cause like I said, my thumb's too stiff to work the hammer.'

'O' course,' Reilly began thoughtfully, 'you don't allus need a thumb,' and level with the end of his sentence, there was a Colt in his right hand spouting flame, as his left hand fanned the hammer.

'I'd sooner drink myse'f to death,' Crane sneered. 'Fanning's a circus trick and all it'll do is get you killed, in a real gunfight.'

'You're wrong, as usual,' Reilly stated flatly. 'Come and take a look.'

'Waal, hell,' Crane spat, as the two men reached the door and the old gunman was able to see the neat group of five shots at heart height in the centre of the board.

'How in hell did you do that?' he demanded.

'You just got to know the trick of it,' Reilly assured his companion. 'See most people, when they're fannin' the hammer of a pistol are so concerned to get off as many shots as they can, they forget to aim,' Reilly went on.

'If'n you just take that split second to line up your target and then ease your palm off'n the hammer real smooth, then you can hit what you aim at, up to mebbe twenty, thirty feet. Against them Ducane pilgrims and around town, that'll be good enough. Takes practice, o'course,' he finished.

Wonderingly, the old man looked at the long-barrelled, worn-butted Remington in his hand. Abruptly, the old gun twirled on its owner's gnarled forefinger, settling easily back into its holster as Crane straightened up. The hard glint was back in his eyes and the glare he threw at Reilly was flat and level and belonged to a man ten years and many drinks younger.

'You got yourse'f a deppity, God help you, Marshal Reilly,' the old gunfighter said softly. 'An' I'll be needin' a month's wages, in advance,' he finished, turning and trudging back to the office.

'Sure,' Reilly offered slyly, at Crane's retreating back. 'What's it for? Drinking money?'

'Cartridges,' the old man said simply, without turning or slowing his pace.

'Get a' plenty,' Reilly ordered and, as

Crane looked his question, the man from Tuscon shrugged. 'Well, I ain't got time to teach the boy to shoot!

'An' Matt,' Reilly finished, 'don't let on what you an' the kid are doin'.'

★　★　★

'I want that bastard marshal hanging from a goddamn tree today and I want that old drunk Crane hanging with him and you can do what ever the hell you want to with the Indian!'

Sirus Ducane paused for breath and, seeing her chance, Rosa stepped smoothly into the breach.

'If we go ridin' in there, Pa, first thing that marshal fella's gonna do is hang Bull,' she offered, barely masking her contempt for the white-haired old man with the mad eyes, who was occupying the high-backed chair behind the littered desk, which stood in the main room of the ranch house.

'He wouldn't dare,' her brother Owen snapped.

'Why not?' Rosa returned simply. 'What would he have to lose? After all,' she finished, with a sneer, 'you can only kill a man once.'

'I could sure make it seem like more'n once!' her brother snarled.

'Rosa's right, as usual.' Stark Ducane, the family's nervous book-keeper put in, eyeing his father with open contempt. 'And this whole thing is getting outa hand.'

'We gotta have that town quiet, Pa,' Stark went on, 'else we got nowhere for Ramirez's men to spend their money and nowhere to hide the Gatl — '

'Shut your goddamn flappin' mouth,' the old man erupted. 'You want the whole goddamn world to know what we're a' doin'?

'Get out. *Get out all of you!*' the old man screamed, clearly having lost all control. '*I can't stand your goddamn faces!*'

★　★　★

73

In the long cool, corridor which separated the two sides of the house and allowed the cool gulf wind free access to it, Rosa found her brother Stark waiting for her later that day, when she returned from issuing orders to the *segundo* Vicente, regarding the watch to be kept on the town.

'He's getting worse,' her slim, Eastern-educated brother began without preamble.

'Tell me about it,' Rosa shrugged, 'but what can we do?'

'We could ease him out of the way, kinda,' Stark began, licking nervous lips as he took the plunge. 'Look, we gotta have Perdition quiet and peaceful, 'cause it's the only place on this coastline where you can get down from the hills. And we can't ship the . . . merchandise from anywhere else.'

'Sure,' Rosa agreed, 'but there ain't no way we can do business without Pa. He's the only one they'll deal with.'

'You ever wonder why that is?' Stark demanded slyly.

'Never give it much thought.' Rosa

shrugged, although little else had occupied her waking thoughts for the past two years.

'There's a book,' Stark began. 'It's got names, dates, all kinds of stuff. He's got letters going back years, all filed and all recorded in this book. If we get that — '

'I . . . I mean . . . we've got it all!' Rosa finished for him.

'We work together in this, Rosa,' her brother warned.

'Don't worry, Stark,' his sister purred, 'I'll see you get what's comin' to you.'

* * *

'What in hell you doin', settin' out on that porch?' Crane demanded. 'Anyone with a rifle could pot you easy from the edge o' town.'

'Sure they could,' Reilly agreed. stretching lazily. 'Only they won't. None of ol' man Ducane's boys can get in without bein' spotted 'cause every kid in town's on the lookout for 'em.

An' Ducane ain't ready for a gunfight yet, not if he thinks he can starve us out. Did you get me a hat?'

'Sure,' Crane admitted, 'but I don't see — '

'Better get stronger spectacles,' Reilly interrupted, rising to his feet.

'Where in hell you goin' now?' Crane demanded, but the man from Tuscon was gone without any reply.

★　★　★

'Now, don't you go gettin fresh, son,' Reilly quietly informed Pecos, as he twisted his boot awkwardly through the stirrup iron so the ankle appeared trapped.

Carefully, Reilly lowered himself to the ground and, keeping a firm grip on the rein, he chirruped to the little pony. Obediently, Pecos edged forward.

'*Help . . . help*,' Reilly screamed as the stirrup iron tightened on his foot and he eased the little pinto to a halt.

Obedient to his orders, at Reilly's

first call, Mangas rounded the corner of the livery barn and was quickly easing Reilly's boot out of the stirrup as the first of the crowd gathered.

'Goddamn jughead,' Reilly swore, ignoring Pecos's disgusted look.

'Jumped afore I was set good. Feels like he broke my damn leg,' Reilly complained.

'It don't feel . . . ' Crane began, feeling cautiously through the boot, as Lauren Wex approached the group.

'Owwwh,' Reilly bellowed. 'Get your goddamn hands off'n me! I can't hardly stand for you to touch it! Get me back to the office an' then you can put a splint on it.'

★ ★ ★

'So mebbe now you two can tell me, what in hell's goin' on?' Crane demanded, as Mangas tied the last loose knot in the bandages encasing Reilly's leg.

'Sure,' Reilly whispered with a grin, 'I broke my leg.'

'You . . . if'n that leg's broke, I'm Geronimo,' Crane managed to snap in a low voice.

'OK,' Reilly whispered, 'I'm gonna make it real plain for you. Bull and his *compadres* jumped me as I was goin' to the cantina, right?'

'Sure,' Crane admitted.

'Only they didn't,' Reilly contradicted himself. 'They didn't jump me. They was set and waitin', like — '

'Like they knew you was comin',' Crane interrupted, with a soft whistle.

'Just like that,' Reilly confirmed. 'I figure someone in town's spyin' for them. It'd make sense, since this town's important to them for some reason. So I aim to . . . uh . . . mislead them a l'il mite.'

'And just how d'you figure to do that?' Crane demanded.

'Waal, first, we're gonna turn Bull's l'il friend loose,' Reilly said. 'Get him in here: I want him to see this,' he finished, pointing to his bandage and splint-encased leg.

78

'It was just as I say, *patron*,' the badly frightened Mexican related. 'He say not to get any smart ideas, 'cause he gonna be sittin' in the jail, with a shotgun an' first sign of trouble an' . . . boom . . . no more Señor Bull. He say Señor Bull will hang as soon as the *federale* judge . . . he get here . . . so it don' matter, anyhow, the man finished, flinching away from the look on the old man's face.

'Goddamn that interferin' son of a bitch,' the old man screeched, hands clawing at the air, as he stood up and strode the length of the big house's broad front veranda where the interview was being conducted. 'I shoulda killed him — ' He stopped abruptly in mid-sentence, and glared back at the terrified Mexican.

'*You!*' he screamed. 'Why are you here? My boy's in jail and you're here walkin' around scot free? Why ain't you dead? What did you think you was wearin' that gun for? I paid you to take care o' him and now he's gonna hang 'cause o' you, you goddamn coward.' Ducane's voice dropped to a sibilant whisper. 'Well, we know how to take care of those who don't do their job.'

'Owen, Vicente,' the old man roared. 'Give this coward Grevas one cartridge. Then you can turn him loose in the mesquite patch.'

★ ★ ★

Up on the rim-rock which bordered the Ducane ranch house, Reilly eased his eyes away from a pair of battered military binoculars and turned to his mute companion.

'What's that all about, Mangas?' he demanded, having watched Owen Ducane check his ornate pistols, before slipping into a patch of mesquite, about an acre in extent, some distance from the back of the house.

'A game,' Mangas signed.

'A game?' Reilly queried. 'And what

in hell are they doin' to that poor bastard?' he asked, as the luckless Mexican was handed a pistol and shoved into an opening in the patch of vegetation.

Eloquently, Mangas pointed to where the man had disappeared, before drawing a cartridge from his belt and holding up a single finger. The significance of the pantomime was not lost on Reilly.

'They give him one cartridge and turn him loose for the other feller to hunt?' Reilly demanded. 'Don't sound like such a sure thing to me,' the man from Tuscon muttered, 'the other feller could easy get lucky.'

★   ★   ★

Down in the mesquite patch, sitting with his back to a tall, wiry tree, Grevas had no illusions about his chances.

Several men had been sentenced to the mesquite in his time there, including his friend, Emilio. Emilio had been very good with both a knife and a pistol and he was as silent in his movements as an Apache. And Owen Ducane had left him in the mesquite patch with both his knees blown off. Grevas had heard him for three days and two nights, until during the third night, blood poisoning or a coyote had ended his suffering.

Ducane was a gunman, not as fast as some the Mexican had seen, but good enough to make Grevas's chances of survival in a straight fight almost nil. He was known to be a poor plainsman, however, and, almost as if to illustrate that, Grevas heard clear sounds of someone moving in the brush a short distance away.

Carefully, he checked his pistol and, after arranging the single cartridge so that it would come under the hammer when he cocked the weapon, the Mexican moved off, working at an angle towards the sounds.

It was almost too easy. Grevas found the gringo waiting behind a bush overlooking one of the myriad narrow trails through the undergrowth, almost where the noise he made had signalled he would be. Without hesitation, the Mexican raised his pistol, simultaneously cocking the weapon.

The slight noise was enough to jerk Ducane round and Grevas sneered. Before the gringo could draw and shoot, he would be dead, the Mexican assured himself as he squeezed the trigger.

7

Up on the rim-rock, the sound of two shots, fired close together, broke the aching, weary silence. Patiently, Reilly scanned the area of mesquite scrub, to be rewarded, a minute or two later, by the sight of Owen Ducane, sauntering out of the patch and making for the house, while, from behind him, there arose the thin scream of a man in mortal agony.

Some change in the wind or a trick of acoustics enabled Reilly to hear the killer's first words.

'Both knees, Pa,' Owen explained, with a self-satisfied nod, 'Wonder how long he'll take . . . ' The rest of the sentence was lost and the man from Tucson motioned Mangas back down the slope to where they had left the horses.

★   ★   ★

Reilly and the boy had slipped out of town in the early evening of the day before Crane had released Grevas. On foot, it had been easy to avoid the sentries posted on the only trail out of town and through the hills.

Quickly arriving at the little canyon which Reilly had located on his first day, they had secured the ponies and equipment Mangas had hidden there and were quickly on their way to the Ducane ranch, where they arrived in time to witness that morning's tragedy.

Neither man spoke as they walked their ponies up the trail which led away from the rim-rock overlooking the ranch buildings and it wasn't until they were riding parallel to the main trail that Reilly spoke.

'Seems to me,' he offered, and his voice was gentle, like the first whispering of a Gulf hurricane, 'that Mr Ducane an' his whelps have lived a mite too long. We'll mebbe have to remedy that there situation, Mangas.'

'Huh,' Mangas grunted, drawing an expressive finger across his throat and then jerking his hand across his body horizontally.

'All of 'em, huh?' the man from Tuscon nodded. 'You're surely right, amigo, an' we better not miss none.'

Followed by Mangas, Reilly turned his pony east, angling away from the main trail to Perdition, more on the chance of finding something than for any other reason, and along towards late afternoon, the pair got lucky.

'What you figure, Mangas?' Reilly asked, looking at the faint twin wheel ruts that signified the passing of a wagon. After a single, intent glance, the Indian looked up the trail.

'Wagon, heavy,' he signed. 'Use trail, many times.'

'Which way?' Reilly demanded, before turning his horse in the direction the other indicated.

★   ★   ★

The day had waned into early evening when Reilly twitched his pony's rein and waited for his companion to draw level.

'There,' he said simply, indicating a substantial building beside a spacious corral, both structures occupying a man-made clearing in the sparse pine forest through which they had been travelling.

Leaving the horses, the two approached the building warily, which turned out to be a large double-doored barn.

Signalling Mangas to wait, Reilly moved forward, the faint moonlight proving sufficient for him to see the characteristic, deep-rutted tracks they had been following, leading up to the door.

Swiftly, Reilly circled the building and, finding the corral empty, moved back to the front and began to ease the nearest of the double doors open.

Darkness greeted him as he stepped into the barn, but a flaring match showed a lantern hanging on its nail near the door and with this alight, Reilly set about investigating the building's contents, which proved mundane enough.

Three sturdy, high-sided freight wagons all but filled the building. Further examination showed them to be slightly modified from the usual run of transport vehicles, in that their iron-shod wheels were nearly double the normal width, while the wagon tongue and harness was modified to allow a team of eight horses to be used, instead of the usual six.

A glance inside showed Reilly that extra planks had also been added to the floor.

'They're movin' somethin' heavy, all right,' the man from Tucson mused, 'but I wonder just what the hell it can be?'

Almost as if in answer to that question, his foot clinked against something in the darkness, but Reilly barely had time to reach down and slip the small, cylindrical object into the pocket of his vest before the double doors were thrown open and a hard voice said, 'You in there, come out where we can see you. An' in case you're thinkin' of tryin' anything fancy, we've got the kid.'

A moment's furious thought showed Reilly that he was clearly out of alternatives, so he snuffed the lantern and moved towards the doors.

'That's far enough, *amigo*,' a second voice said in heavily accented English.

'Chavez,' the first voice ordered, 'get in there and get a coupla lanterns lit. Let's see what we've caught.'

A figure, clearly Mexican by his costume, scuttled into the barn. A match flared and a lantern subsequently bloomed into flame, drawing a whistle from the lanky gunman who now moved into the barn behind a long-barrelled Colt.

'Well, well,' the white man sneered. 'Look who we got here, the big he-bull hisse'f.'

''Evenin', Marshal,' the gunman

went on drily. 'You sure heal quick; that leg don't hardly look broke at all.'

Thumbs hooked into his belt. Reilly spat carefully in the dust. 'Let the kid go,' he began, letting the whine creep into his voice.

'Oh no, I don't think we can do that,' the man said. 'We wouldn't know who the l'il bastard might go runnin' off to.'

'*Monterey*,' he bellowed, 'get that kid in here.'

Almost instantly a dishevelled Mangas, minus his treasured gunbelt, was shoved roughly into the barn. The boy lost his footing and stumbled to his knees, shaking his head as if to clear it. Reilly saw the boy's fist clenched sideways in the dirt, the time-worn Mimbreños signal of a brave heart electing for the warpath.

A second white man, tall and fat, lurched clumsily through the doorway after the youngster, followed by another Mexican.

Four then, and one, maybe two, with the horses, Reilly calculated swiftly, easing his hands minutely towards his guns, as the big white man reached down to grab a handful of hair and jerk Mangas to his feet.

But the young Apache came up quickly of his own accord, twisting and slamming a sinewy knee up between the man's legs, doubling him over as, in a smooth continuation of the same move, Mangas jerked loose the other's Colt and drove a bullet into the big man's chest, drawing the attention of the other three Ducane men away from Reilly.

Desperately, the boy tried to cock the heavy revolver, but by the time his weapon was ready, it was all over.

The sound of Mangas's first shot had barely died away before Reilly was moving, worn Colts flickering from their holsters in a chain lightning draw.

His first bullet drove into the chest of the gunman who had been doing all the talking, driving him backwards, dead before he hit the ground, while his second and third slammed into the head of the fourth Mexican standing just inside the door.

Without waiting to see the result of his shooting, Reilly vaulted a bale of straw as Chavez's bullet whisked past his head, dropped behind it and threw a shot into the Mexican's chest almost simultaneously. Chavez folded as Reilly bellowed, 'Get out of the light, kid.' Mangas, Apache quick, threw himself in a rolling dive behind the wall of the barn as a bullet pecked the straw where he had been standing barely a moment before.

Swiftly, Reilly joined the boy, edging carefully around in front of him. Reaching up, he turned out the only lantern left alight, plunging the barn into darkness.

'I'm gonna finish this *hombre*,' he whispered, drawing Mangas's ear next to his mouth. 'I figure there's only one,' Reilly went on, shoving his left-hand Colt into the youngster's hand. 'So after I go, you count your fingers on one hand twice, slow, then heave that lantern into the brush. Then sit tight.

Don't start movin' around outside, 'cause I ain't gonna be askin' questions afore I shoot.' With that, the man from Tucson was gone with no more sound than a shadow in the moonlight.

Once outside, Reilly eased himself carefully erect, hugging the dark contours of the building, as he carefully counted down the time.

Without warning, a heavy object crashed into the brush nearby but Reilly was ready and almost level with the sound. Then he launched himself across the intervening space to land heavily in the brush beyond.

Instantly, he began to roll, following the crashing, tearing noise which the last Ducane man had made in approaching him, when, suddenly, he was brought to a halt by the substantial trunk of a large pine tree.

Breathing a swift sigh of relief, Reilly wriggled behind it, palming his Colt as he shifted noiselessly to lie prone amongst the dark pine needles, all the while listening intently to the clumsy progress of the man hunting him.

Suddenly, a darker shadow loomed against the lightless wall of pine trees and Reilly, who lived by his own curious morality, called softly, in the liquid Spanish of the Border.

'Drop your gun, *mi compadre*, or you're a dead man.'

His answer was the deafening roar of a pistol and, aiming at the flash, Reilly replied instantly, firing twice. He was rewarded by a loud thud, accompanied by a momentary scuffling.

Patiently, Reilly waited and, after several minutes, he crawled forward noiselessly, feeling in front of him with his pistol. Moments later, the muzzle of his weapon touched a solid object, which investigation proved to be the boot of his victim, the flacidity of the body and sticky mess which was the man's chest confirming that he was beyond any sort of earthly help.

Ignoring the dead man, Reilly moved swiftly through the darkness, following his ears and his nose, to be rewarded within minutes by the gentle clinking of a bridle chain and the uneasy whiffle of a horse.

* * *

Mangas was waiting patiently with his back to a post of the corral, when the two-note call of a whippoorwill sounded from the screen of pine in front of him. Swiftly, the youngster wriggled behind the post, before softly answering and then noiselessly shifting position.

'Glad to see you ain't gettin' careless, boy,' a mild voice said out of the darkness behind him, 'but you might wanta remember how good a man shows up against that light-coloured sand,' Reilly explained, as he appeared, apparently from out of the surrounding earth. 'Here, you might want this,' he finished, carefully passing across the boy's holstered Colt and accepting his own weapon in return.

'Don't forget to check the loads and

the action,' Reilly ordered, turning to trudge towards the barn. 'Never trust a gun that's been out of your sight.'

'How many with the horses?' the boy signed clumsily, as he slipped his treasured weapon away.

'One,' Reilly answered shortly. 'Had to kill 'im, wouldn't have it no other way.'

'Two shots,' the boy signed, imitating a pistol with his fingers by way of a question.

'Sure,' Reilly explained. 'It was dark and all I could see was his gun flash. So I shot both sides of it, in case he was left handed. An' afore you ask,' Reilly went on abruptly, 'it's thinkin' o' things like that that keeps a man alive. You better get the habit.'

8

'Somethin' about what that first fella said's been botherin' me,' Reilly began, as the pair moved through the door and surveyed the body-strewn interior.

'He weren't surprised to see me here at all, and how'd he know I was supposed to have a broken leg? Didn't have time to get here from the ranch and, anyhow, their tracks are comin' from the wrong direction. I'm sayin' it wouldn't hurt none, mebbe, to search them bodies.'

'Fresh Bull Durham,' Reilly said later, pointing to the bright yellow sack of tobacco which lay amongst the collection of objects their search had revealed.

'Store bought,' he went on. 'Yesterday or day before at the latest. And the only place close enough for him to have got it was Henry Vance's store in Perdition. O' course,' he added thoughtfully, just 'cause he's carryin' it, don't mean he bought it hisself . . .

'See if you can scare up some coal-oil,' Reilly ordered, gathering up the objects of his search after a moment's thought, 'I'll get us some firewood. We may as well give Mr Ducane something else to think about,' he explained and, as the young Apache looked his question, Reilly asked innocently, 'Got a match?'

* * *

'Well, that sure enough tears it,' Crane snapped, when Reilly quietly told him about the burning of the barn and its contents. 'If'n he weren't gonna kill you before, he sure as shootin' will now.'

'Sure,' Reilly agreed, 'but not for a while. Them wagons was fresh greased. Whatever he's movin', he's movin' it soon. And that,' the man from Tucson finished, easing himself down into the squeaky, uncomfortable office chair, 'presents something of a problem, as the cottontail said when he saw his friend caught in the rabbit trap.

'Anyone come visitin' while we was gone?' Reilly continued mildly.

'Sure,' came the innocent reply, 'Henry dropped in some cartridges. Coupla others . . . oh and Miz Wex looked in to see how your leg was. She seemed kinda worried, so I told her how your leg wasn't bust. That was all right, weren't it?' Crane bridled, seeing the look on Reilly's face. 'Damn it, Fargo, she's the *alcalde*!' he snapped.

'That's right, Matt,' Reilly replied thoughtfully, 'she is, isn't she?'

* * *

'But what in hell can we do?' Stark Ducane whined pathetically, kicking at a half-burnt, steel-rimmed wheel, which was all that remained recognizable of the secret barn and its contents.

'Do? *Do?*' Old man Ducane roared. 'Them guns has gotta be moved!

Adams'll be off the inlet a week from now and if they ain't there, he'll head back to Galveston and I'll be out about two hundred thousand dollars. Not to mention the biggest chance this family'll ever have to really be something in this Godforsaken country.'

'Take it easy, Pa,' Rosa Ducane snapped contemptuously. 'As long as the guns are safe, we can easy scare up some more transport.'

'Them wagons was specially built to take the weight,' Stark Ducane put in, voice rising again towards a whine.

'But wagons ain't the only way to move guns. What d'you think, Wes?' she demanded abruptly, turning to her laconic elder brother.

'Two wagons, mebbe, for the . . . uh . . . special . . . uh . . . stuff . . . ' Wes Ducane began hesitantly, with an anxious eye on his father. 'Move the rifles and shells by pack mules.'

'We got enough stock to do that?' Owen demanded.

'About half what we need,' his

brother admitted uneasily.

'All right,' Rosa began, momentarily forgetful of her father, 'this is what we'll do . . . '

Her reminder came swiftly, with all the arrogance to be expected of Sirus Ducane.

'And just when in hell did you become head o' this family?' the old man screamed uncontrollably.

'I just thought — ' his daughter began.

'You ain't got the necessary equipment for that,' the old man sneered. 'Best leave thinkin' to the men!'

'All right, Pa,' Stark Ducane began contemptuously, 'just what are we gonna do?'

Without warning, the old man sprang forward and backhanded his son hard across the mouth, knocking him to the ground. Stark looked up to find himself staring into the muzzle of a pistol, below a pair of eyes which were hardly less menacing in their emptiness.

'Don't think you can sass me, boy.'

101

the old man snarled, ''cause blood kin or no, I'll kill you where you stand.'

'An' as for the rest of you,' Sirus Ducane roared, rounding on the group, 'when I decide what I want you to do, I'll goddamn let you know!

'Now get the hell back to the ranch,' the old man ordered, swinging aboard his giant white stallion. 'I'm expectin' a visitor.'

'Hell, the ol' bastard's gettin' worse by the day,' Wes Ducane muttered, as he turned away. 'One day we're sure gonna pay for it.'

'Mebbe, one day,' Rosa responded, having heard as she came up behind him, 'he won't be runnin' things. In the meantime, start movin' the stuff from Perdition, down to the main cave.'

'But Pa said — ' her brother began.

'He ain't gonna know, Wes,' she interrupted. 'An' if we don't start movin' it now, we'll never do it,' she went on, seeing his doubtful look as he turned to carry out her instructions, ''cause we ain't got enough stock. You said so yourself.'

'OK, Rosa, you're the boss,' her brother acknowledged reluctantly.

'Not yet,' the girl snarled at his retreating back, 'but give it time, just a l'il time. An' I just wonder who's comin' way out here to see you?' she went on thoughtfully, turning to stare after the departing figure of her father.

★ ★ ★

Next day, along about first drink time, Reilly and Crane were conducting their habitual check of the town, when Reilly stopped abruptly and pushed back his wide-brimmed sombrero.

'Why, hell,' he began, 'if I ain't a ring-tailed idjut.'

'I ain't arguing,' Crane put in complacently, turning to eye his friend, 'but just what brings you to that there conclusion this time?'

''Cause I been lookin' at this whole set-up back-asswards,' Reilly explained.

'We know Ducane's movin' somethin',

somethin' heavy,' the man from Tucson went on, 'but the question we ain't asked ourselves is . . . why? Why go to the trouble of movin' it from here?'

'Seems easy enough to me, now you put it that way,' Crane said thoughtfully. 'It's something illegal and too hard to move in the States without someone nosy, like the Texas Rangers, asking questions. Question is, o' course, how'd they get the stuff, whatever it is, south of the border in the first place?'

'Depends what it is, but it'd be simple enough,' Reilly considered. 'You could move the stuff in small amounts. That way it's not difficult to hide.'

'Or . . . ' he went on thoughtfully, 'you could bring it all through some l'il town, in the Badlands, where you figure there ain't no law.'

'Like Dragon Wells?' Crane offered, having heard the story of the massacre from Reilly.

'It's possible.' Reilly shrugged. 'But you're forgettin' another question. Smugglin' from here ain't that much easier than from Texas. There's a fair slew of law down here. What about the *Rurales*?'

'What about 'em?' Crane demanded.

'They ain't stupid,' Reilly explained. 'An' one o' their patrols is bound to have picked sign o' what Ducane's doin'. An' once they'd done that, how long you figure it'd take them to work out what was goin' on and stop it?'

'They've been paid off, then,' Crane stated matter-of-factly.

'Sure,' Reilly acknowledged. 'Only somethin' as big as this, Ducane's smart enough to pay off the man at the top, then let him take care of the small fry. Probably be cheaper, too. An' I just wonder who that might be? An' just what's in it for him?' the man from Tucson went on thoughtfully.

'What you figure they're smugglin', Fargo?' the old gunman went on before the other could go any further.

'Guns: only thing it could be,' his companion stated flatly, delving into a pocket and finally bringing to light the object he had found in the barn.

'Ever seen a cartridge like that?' Reilly asked mildly, after a brief explanation of where he had found it.

'Long way too big for a pistol,' Crane began doubtfully, minutely examining the empty case. 'And it's pretty big for a rifle . . . '

'Look at the end,' Reilly instructed and when Crane had done as instructed, his companion went on. 'See them marks? They was made by the extractor mechanism of a Gatling gun,' Reilly explained.

'A Gatling? Christ, you mean Sirus Ducane is runnin' Gatlin' guns?' Crane bellowed, startled out of his usual self-control.

'Sure, that's right, tell everybody!' Reilly snapped. 'An' don't be too sure that there ain't somethin' more behind it,' he finished softly.

'But Jesus, Fargo, where in hell did Sirus get a Gatling gun?' the old gunman demanded.

'I figure, like you said, that it's Gatling *guns*. An' if I knew that,' Reilly responded pityingly, 'the old bastard'd be in prison and I'd be sittin' in on the big game in Sundance Wilson's in Tucson, takin' it easy.

'As it is,' he went on, with some asperity, 'that's somethin' we're gonna have to find out for ourselves. Along about sundown, get Mangas and our rifles, I'll meet you at the livery barn.'

'Where we goin'?' Crane demanded.

'Oh, just a l'il social call,' Reilly said whimsically.

From behind a nearby building, where she had heard almost everything, the slim figure of Lauren Wex emerged.

For a moment, a glare of hatred lit her face as her gaze followed the two men, then she whisked about and was gone, heading for a certain run-down adobe in the town's sprawling Mexican quarter.

★ ★ ★

'This may end up being a real unsocial call,' Crane grumbled as he glared down at the main building of the Ducane ranch, in the rapidly fading twilight of the following day.

'Quit complainin',' Reilly said easily, 'An' anyhow, figure this, at least there ain't no way you can die young, you ol' fossil, whereas me and the boy, why we — '

'Shut up, you damn idjut,' Crane snarled. 'And Fargo,' he went on softly, as his two friends were about to slip away into the beckoning darkness, 'be careful. You an' the boy'll be a long time dyin' if Owen Ducane catches you.'

*　*　*

'*Nada*,' Reilly whispered disgustedly, having completed his search of the ranch's outbuildings and joined Mangas at their agreed rendezvous, in the dense shadow of one of the larger horse barns.

'Guess we'll just have to sashay over and try the big house, though I can't see them Ducanes hidin' guns there,' Reilly muttered doubtfully. 'Leastways,

I'm gonna prospect the place,' he decided abruptly, addressing his companion. 'You stay here, back me up if I hit trouble.'

Carefully tilting forward the wide-brimmed sombrero, which he had appropriated, together with a greasy poncho from a member of the ranch crew, whom they had left securely tied and sleeping off his headache in a convenient dry wash, Reilly moved out of the welcome shadow of the horse barn and began to saunter casually in the direction of the ranch's sprawling, whitewashed main house.

The night being warm, most of the windows were open and Reilly began a casual circuit of the building, stopping occasionally to listen.

At the back of the house, a large paved veranda had been built and, as Reilly approached it, he suddenly stiffened into immobility, desperately seeking the shadows thrown by the wall, the ripple of voices having told him that the veranda was clearly occupied.

Cautiously he crept forward until, suddenly, Sirus Ducane's whisky-slurred tones assailed his ears.

'I tell you, Chico,' the old man was saying, 'your boss, Señor El Presidente is gettin' greedy. I bin givin' that ol' bastard ten per cent clean off the top for years. Then he tries to stiff me for twenty. Tell you, Chico, when a man, 'specially an *el presidente*, starts gettin' greedy, it's time for him to go.'

'My sentiments exactly, Señor Ducane,' agreed a cultured voice, in perfect English. 'But to come to the details . . . ?'

'Guns'll be delivered to the place we agreed, but from there it's up to you. How you figure to play it?'

'It will be verra simple,' the silky voice explained. 'El Presidente Martinez and his *compañeros* . . . eh . . . amuse themselves in the new presidential palace every evening, usually until daylight. My men, armed with your rifles, will surround the place.' The voice went on, an edge of cruelty now colouring its words. 'The guards will be either bribed or killed and then Martinez and his men will be . . . ah . . . *accidentally* shot while trying to escape.'

'An' the new president will be . . . ?' Ducane sneered.

'Me.' the silky voice said, with complete self-assurances 'Domingo Velasquez, President of Mexico, elected on a ticket to help the poor, suffering, down-trodden peasants — '

'An' we split the pickin's fifty-fifty?' Ducane interrupted with a snarl.

'But, of course, *mi amigo*, how else?'

But Velaquez's flowery assurance was interrupted as a hard voice said loudly from the vicinity of Reilly's left ear, 'Well, well, look who's come a visitin'. So nice when folks drop in unexpected.'

Reilly twisted desperately, hands driving under his poncho for his weapons, but something smashed into the side of his head forcing him, half conscious, to his knees, from where a second blow tipped him into a merciful oblivion.

9

'How much you figure he heard, Pa?' said a feminine voice, breaking into Reilly's head as his mind surfaced through the waves of nausea.

'Too damn much!' Owen Ducane snarled, as Reilly, forcing his eyes to slits, swiftly scanned his immediate vicinity.

Two men and a woman stood in front of the big desk which dominated the centre of the untidy, furniture-cluttered main room of what was clearly the Ducane ranch house, while Sirus Ducane occupied his normal place behind it. Beyond that, Reilly could see no one else and, after a moment's consideration, he decided his unconsciousness should continue indefinitely.

'So what are we gonna do with him, Pa?' the girl repeated, 'You figure he's the governor's man you was tellin' us about?'

'Don't matter one way or t'other,' Owen Ducane snapped, with a hint of eagerness. 'We can't leave him alive. He's for the mesquite, ain't he, Pa?'

'Sure,' the old man nodded approvingly. 'Only you and Vicente both are goin' after him. Now get him outa here.'

'But, Pa.' Reilly heard the younger Ducane's voice begin to rise as he was picked up and dragged outside. 'I don' need Vicente! I can take that bastard . . . ' and the slamming of the solid door drew a veil over the rest of Owen Ducane's whining.

It soon became obvious to Reilly that his captors were taking no chances with him, when he was thrown into a small, flat-roofed building with thick adobe walls and a substantial door. His hands and feet were left free and, thankful for small mercies, Reilly waited for the sound of footsteps to die away before he began a noiseless survey of his prison.

What he found wasn't encouraging.

The door was a good tight fit in the frame, secured on the outside by what felt like bolts as well as a robust lock. There were no windows or other openings of any kind and, plainly, the Ducanes had clear ideas about handling dangerous prisoners.

Reilly had barely finished a detailed examination of his prison, when a scrabbling at the door revealed the presence of one of his guards.

Hastily, he dropped to the floor, closing his eyes as he did so. He was barely in time because, moments later, the door was thrust open, a heavy body flung into the little room and a familiar voice bellowed, 'Goddamn you greaser bastards! If I had my guns I'd make you skunks hard to locate. Come back here, you puling . . . '

Reilly listened in admiration as the diatribe continued for a full minute, with barely a repetition, only stopping as the speaker clearly ran out of breath and imagination.

'The more genteel aspects o' your eddication sure have been neglected, Matt,' Reilly offered softly.

'Fargo! Christ alive! I thought they'd got you sure, boy!' Crane blurted.

'Nope,' Reilly admitted, 'but I ain't exactly optimistic about our chances. Where's Mangas?'

'Ain't sure,' the other admitted, 'and its worrying the hell outa me.'

As if in answer to Reilly's question, a thin agonized scream split the night and almost immediately a knock sounded on the door of their prison.

'You hear that, *amigos*?' a coarse, sneering voice enquired. 'That's your little Apache *compadre*. Señor Owen, he is ... eh ... having a l'il fun with him, I thin'.'

'Christ, you goddamn bastards,' Crane flared instantly. 'He ain't nothin' but a kid. Christ, Fargo, ain't there nothin' we can do?'

'No,' Reilly said softly, 'nothin'. Except hope he'll die like an Apache. Now leave it. Get some sleep.'

115

'Sleep! Christ Almighty! How can you . . . ?' Crane began vehemently.

'Because we're gonna need it. On account o' we may be next on the menu,' Reilly answered shortly, drawing up his long legs to sit with his back against the wall and beginning to roll the inevitable cigarette.

For a moment Crane stood undecided then, realizing the sense of Reilly's suggestion, flung himself full length on the dirt floor.

He was just drifting off to sleep when Reilly's voice, speaking in low guttural Apache, broke into his consciousness.

The words were in the deep-throated Mimbreños dialect and, as Crane listened, catching a word here and there, the hair began to rise on the back of his neck. He had heard these words once before, when a long dead chief mourned over the body of his son, pointlessly tortured and killed by a group of white buffalo hunters.

Reilly was swearing the revenge oath of the Mimbreño Apache, the oath a man swears over a relative or lodge brother, the oath he swears when he means to kill or die.

*   *   *

'We got a li'l surprise for you, Marshal,' Owen Ducane sneered, when Reilly and his deputy were led out of their prison early the next morning. 'I believe this is a friend of yours,' he went on, motioning forward two of his father's *vaqueros*, who were supporting someone between them while Vicente, the Ducane *segundo* sauntered along carelessly behind.

More correctly it should have been *something*, because what remained of Mangas could scarcely have been described as human.

'What have you done to him?' Reilly asked softly, and though not a muscle of his face moved, there was death in his voice.

'Well, to start with we busted both his knees and his elbows, so's he

117

couldn't run,' Ducane began conversationally. 'Then, I started in to skin him, though I ain't very good at it yet. Still, practice makes perfect, or so folk say. Then Vicente cut off his . . .

'He's still alive by the way,' Ducane finished, coming to the end of his description of Mangas's ordeal. 'So we're gonna string him up over there, where he can see what's gonna happen to you an' this ol' bastard.'

'So what've you cowards got lined up for me an' this ol' fool?' Reilly began, initiating the plan he and Crane had devised the night before.

'Ain't no call to go talkin' about me like that, Marshal,' Crane whined in senile protest, before anyone else could respond, sounding as though he was on the verge of tears. 'Ain't my fault they caught your tame Apache dog.'

'Shut your goddamn mouth, you stupid old bastard,' Reilly snarled. 'That goddamn Indian ain't no more use than you are!'

Crane relapsed into a sullen, senile

mumbling, affecting not to notice the grins around him. All eyes were on Reilly and, observing this, the old gunman moved backwards until he was standing next to a fat *vaquero*, who had appropriated his twin Remingtons. Crane came to a halt just out of the man's eyeline and settled back to wait. Now it all depended on Reilly.

'You ain't exactly popular with people, are you, Mr Marshal?' Owen Ducane began with a sneer. 'You might find you need a friend before you get through.'

'What I don't need is advice from a yellow whelp, who'd sell the straw outa his mother's kennel, if'n he knew who she was,' Reilly said spitefully.

'Give him his gun and a cartridge and let's get this over with. You better explain it to him, girl,' Sirus Ducane ordered abruptly, before his incensed son could reply.

'Now listen, Marshal,' Rosa began, 'this is the setup. You get your Colt and one cartridge. Usually, it's only Owen who you're up against, but we figure

119

'cause you're meant to be pretty good with a short gun, that Vicente'd better help him out — '

'Like I said,' Reilly interrupted, 'yella as mustard. Still it ain't surprisin', seein' whose whelp he is.'

'You better watch your mouth, *amigo*,' Vicente, the Ducane *segundo*, put in, pointing to the acre-wide patch of mesquite, 'a man can be a long time dyin' out there.'

'I'll bear it in mind, greaser.' Reilly sneered back.

'Anyhow,' Rosa went on, 'Owen and Vicente go in first, then you're goin' five minutes later, from the other side. Last man standin' is the winner.'

'What happens to me if I win?' Reilly demanded.

'Don't worry, Marshal, you won't!' the girl laughed pityingly.

★ ★ ★

Once released into the mesquite patch, Reilly moved deep enough into the scrubby, head-high vegetation to ensure his movements could not be observed from outside, then turned abruptly left and broke into a noiseless run.

A minute later, he was squatting with his back to a narrow trunk, making a swift but thorough examination of the weapon he'd been given.

It turned out to be one of his own Colts and, having worked the action and examined the mechanism, it was clear that the pistol had not been altered or damaged in any way.

'That'd be too obvious, I guess, even for them coyotes,' Reilly muttered, 'but I sure am wonderin' about this cartridge.'

It didn't take Reilly long to discover the trick the Ducanes had been playing on their victims.

'Reloaded,' Reilly confirmed to himself, having seen the scratches on the case made by recrimping, 'but they left out the powder,' he went on, one twist of his powerful fingers having served to twist the slug out of its seat.

'Well, I guess at least we know where

we are,' Reilly told himself, rising and moving silently into the brush, as certain suspicious sounds reached his ears. 'Now I wonder just how smart that greaser *segundo* really is?'

* * *

'*Tsst*,' Vicente hissed, pausing with upraised pistol cocked and ready in his hand, at the sight of the plain, fresh tracks which crossed the narrow trail he had been following.

'This is gonna be a cinch,' Ducane muttered, moving up beside the Mexican, 'All we do is just follow his tracks and shoot the bastard.'

'Mebbe that what he want us to thin',' Vicente lisped doubtfully. 'Mebbe he leave this track for us to follow, while he wait and shoot us when we go past.'

'But he ain't got nothin' to shoot with!' Ducane protested.

'No; we don' take no chances with this one,' the *segundo* replied thoughtfully. 'I thin' we work along next to these tracks, just in case the gringo, he is bein' verra smart.'

'There he is!' Ducane hissed, pointing ahead to where the crown of a battered Stetson showed above a particularly impenetrable mesquite thicket.

The two men had found a narrow path which seemed to run parallel with the one Reilly had taken and, following it carefully, they had eventually been rewarded with what appeared to be an easy target.

'I'm going round this way,' Ducane went on, motioning with his pistol. 'When I get set, I'll whistle and then we can blast him from both sides.'

To Vicente, the waiting seemed interminable, until suddenly a piercing, two-note whistle split the air. Without hesitation, the Mexican emptied his left-hand pistol into the brush beneath where the crown of the hat showed, carefully spacing his shots to take into account any movement by his victim.

Unbelievably, Reilly's head gear remained fixed, apparently immovably, in the position that the two men had first seen it.

Vicente, however, was given no time for further speculation.

'Turn around, greaser,' a mild voice said behind him, 'but be real careful what you do with your hands. That way you may just live a l'il longer.'

Carefully keeping his hands well clear of his weapons, Vicente turned gingerly on his heels. A sneer of contempt spread across his face as he saw that his opponent's pistol was still thrust in his belt.

'Fill your hand, you yeller greaser bastard,' Reilly ordered softly, 'you just done run out your string.'

And, level with his last word, both men's hands were driving for their weapons.

10

'What in hell's takin' them so long?' Sirus Ducane snarled irritably, for perhaps the tenth time in as many minutes. This time, however, as if in answer to his question, there came the crack of two shots, sounding so close together as to appear one.

'Damn good,' Ducane sneered, receiving confirmatory nods and grins from his obsequious offspring and employees.

'Owen, Vicente!' he went on, raising his voice to a shout. 'Leave the bastard to rot and get the hell out here! We got work to do!'

But minute followed minute without the reappearance of either man and Ducane was just drawing breath to give vent to another bellow, when there was a rustle from the mesquite directly in front of his position and Owen Ducane was thrust through into the blazing south-western sunlight.

Gone, however, was the cocky self-assurance, lost somewhere along with the fancy sombrero and the silver-mounted Colts.

Bare-headed and white-faced, the youngest member of the Ducane clan was ejected from the all-enveloping mesquite, an arm round his throat pulling him backwards and off balance, while the muzzle of a battered Colt ground up under his chin.

'If'n you want this worthless piece o' trash back in one piece,' a hard voice said from the thicket behind the youngest Ducane, 'shuck your belts and do it pronto!'

For a moment stillness reigned, to be broken by Sirus Ducane.

'He never was worth the food he ate,' the old man said thoughtfully, 'so I guess you can have him. Get the — '

'Now I guess you'd better think real careful about that,' a cold voice said close to the old man's ear, interrupting his order and sending an icy chill down his back as he heard the deadly, aching lust to kill beneath the words.

Unseen by anyone else, as soon as Ducane appeared, Crane had acted.

In a single lightning movement, he had snatched his guns from the belt of the *vaquero* wearing them and mercilessly laid the man's head open with a skilfully wielded pistol.

The two men between him and the elder Ducane were dispatched with similar lightning ruthlessness and, before any of the gang could make a move, the old man had taken a single long step which placed him behind his victim.

'Get up here, Fargo,' the old man snapped, grinding the muzzle of his pistol into Ducane's spine by way of reminder, 'and bring that dog dirt with you.'

'Now, you and me are goin' for a l'il ride, Sirus,' Crane resumed conversationally, as Reilly and his prisoner began to ascend the slope rapidly. 'Back up and be real careful.'

But Ducane had barely taken a single step before two of his men, thinking themselves blocked from Crane's line of vision, went for their guns. The old lawman didn't hesitate.

Dropping to one knee, his left hand flickered across his body, the palm snapping back the hammer of the battered Remington, driving his first shot into the nearest man before his victim's weapon had cleared leather.

Smoothly controlling the big pistol's recoil, Crane snapped his second into the head of the other gunman, throwing him backwards, his pistol exploding harmlessly into the dust.

'Nobody told you to stop movin', Sirus,' Crane snarled, coming creakily erect as Reilly joined the pair, still with Owen Ducane held in his iron grip.

'Get the boy, Matt,' Reilly ordered, 'we ain't leavin' him to the likes o' these.'

'He's dead, Fargo,' Crane called bitterly, after a swift examination. 'Don't hardly see how he lived as long as he did after what this scum done to him.'

'He was a good man, that's why,' Reilly answered softly, and the red killing light flared in his eyes as he raised his pistol and said almost thoughtfully, 'Mebbe we should send some o' this filth to keep him company on the trail to the Land o' Good Huntin'.

'An' I think we should start with you, Mr Ducane,' Reilly finished softly, bringing up his Colt smoothly to line the muzzle between the old man's eyes.

Looking into those icy-blue eyes behind the yawning bore of Reilly's pistol, fear, raw and undiluted, penetrated Ducane's megalomania for perhaps the first time in years and it was with an aching flood of relief that he heard Crane say, 'Ain't one of 'em fit to lick the dust off'n his moccasins, Fargo. Best we get outa here. There'll be other times.'

'Guess you're right,' Reilly acknowledged, but his reluctance was palpable as he lowered his weapon and snapped, 'Get movin', Mr Ducane. Up to the corral. We're all gonna take a l'il ride.'

'The rest of you just stay where you are,' Crane ordered, 'and you, boy,' he went on, gesturing at a youngster in the front of the crowd, 'bring me my belt. Oh . . . and the marshal's too.'

★   ★   ★

Having reached the corral, the work of saddling the horses and strapping on their gunbelts was swiftly completed and Crane was about to climb aboard, when Reilly stopped him.

'Saddle one for Mr Ducane, Matt. We're takin' him along for life insurance.'

'I ain't . . . ' Ducane began, but a minute lifting of Reilly's pistol brought silence like the grave.

Still grasping the youngest of the Ducane clan by the neck, Reilly waited until Crane had completed his task and swung into the saddle, winding the reins of Ducane's mount around his saddle horn as he did so.

'Mount up,' the man from Tucson ordered, a single imperious flick of his Colt in the older Ducane's direction emphasizing his order.

But, as Ducane reluctantly shoved a foot into the stirrup and heaved himself upright, a shot rang out from the crowd, slicing into his back, level with the heart, and tumbling him limp and lifeless to the ground.

For a second there was only stunned silence, before Owen Ducane jerked both elbows backwards, breaking Reilly's hold.

'Get them!' he screamed shrilly, throwing himself to the ground.

Reilly's hands suddenly became a flickering blur, as he emptied his Colt in the general direction of the crowd.

Ducane's riders scattered wildly, and Reilly dropped below the belly of his restless horse, rolling between the animal's legs, then rising instantly with the pony's body between him and the guns of the gang.

In one swift movement he was astride and spurring his mount. Crane waited a single instant to see his companion safely away, before setting spurs to his own wild-eyed pony and tearing after him, followed by the mount they had intended for the late and unlamented Sirus Ducane.

Bullets pecked around the fleeing pair and they seemed set to escape the ranch unscathed, when, suddenly, a slug, better aimed or luckier than the rest, tore into the rib cage of Crane's mount and on into the heart, killing the animal instantly.

Kicking free of the stirrups at the first impact, the old gunman left the saddle in a horse-breaker's roll, landing in the dirt of the trail, bruised but unharmed.

Without hesitation, Crane staggered to his feet, dragging out his pistols, more than ready to sell his life as dearly as he could to ensure his friend's escape. Awkwardly cocking both weapons, he promised himself grimly that he would have plenty of company when he finally took the warrior's road, west of the sunset.

He needn't have bothered.

The leading group of Ducane men was barely a hundred yards distant, with Crane grimly figuring ranges, when a horse turned in front on him, in a blinding flurry of dust and an angry voice snapped irritably, 'Get up here, you damned ol' fool! Ain't losin' no more deppities today!'

Crane found his wrist gripped by a sinewy hand as he was all but dragged aboard the savage little cow pony, which was instantly hauled around in a rumpscraping turn and goaded up the trail.

'This here is a good l'il pony,' Crane shouted into the wind, 'but he ain't gonna be able to keep this up for long, carryin' double.'

As if in response, the little beast crested the last rise of the trail, hiding the pair from their pursuers.

'Off!' Reilly snapped and, as Crane

obeyed instantly, sliding into the dust, his companion jerked loose the rope from his saddle and, in almost the same motion, built a loop and dropped it over the head of the pony they had intended for Sirus Ducane, which as soon as it was out of the sound of gunfire had paused to graze.

'If'n you're waitin' for a invite, Matt . . . ' Reilly began, but Crane was in the saddle almost as soon as the words left his companion's mouth, casting off the loop, turning the little pony and leading their escape at a dead run.

★ ★ ★

Back at the Ducane main house, Rosa Ducane turned away from her brother's hysterical preparations for pursuing the fugitives and signalled to one of her late father's gunmen.

'Find Señor Velasquez,' she ordered. 'Explain to him that he and I need to talk a little . . . business.'

Momentarily, the man hesitated, but one look into those mad eyes, suddenly so like her father's, was all he needed.

'*Sí, señorita*,' he acknowledged simply, and turned to obey.

It seemed the identity of the new boss of Ranchero Ducane had already been decided.

★   ★   ★

'Waal, waal, talk about fools for luck!' Reilly whistled softly, as he examined the imprints of the tracks he had found on the broad trail, around about sunset of the day he and Crane had escaped the Ducane ranch by the skin of their teeth.

'Hey, Matt, come an' look at this an' then tell me that we ain't runnin' in luck today,' Reilly called.

Crane left the little rise where he had been lying to survey their back trail and joined his companion.

'Luck!' he began disgustedly, 'Did I hear you say we was runnin' in luck?

Jesus, Fargo,' the old man went on, 'we ain't got a dozen cartridges between us, no grub, less water, an' them ponies is just about played out.'

'Is that all?' Reilly asked straight-faced, 'Hell, Matt, you sure worry worse than an ol' woman.'

'No, goddamn it, that ain't all,' the old man erupted. 'There's a bunch of mebbe a dozen riders followin' us and we ain't much more than an hour in front of them. And what is it that's got you so all fired interested?'

With the air of a conjuror demonstrating a new trick, Reilly indicated the patch of sand he had been examining.

'Wagon tracks,' he said succinctly, 'but not just any wagon.' he went on, 'Ducane's wagon, the one I burnt. And they was carrying something heavy.'

'So what?' Crane demanded, glaring anxiously over his shoulder. 'On this trail they could be headin' for that barn.'

'Nope,' Reilly stated emphatically. 'They're goin' away from the barn, heading in that direction,' he went on, gesturing vaguely into the blue distance. 'And you know what's over there, don't you. l'il Matty?' Reilly demanded patronizingly.

'Hell, no,' Crane snarled. 'Suppose you spit out whatever's stickin' in your craw?'

'Over there,' Reilly continued easily, 'is the sea. With big ships, that'll carry lots of guns, wherever you want to take them.'

'That's real interestin', Fargo, and surely worth lookin' into, but just right now, we mebbe got somethin' else we oughta be thinkin' on!' Crane retorted irritably.

'Sure,' Reilly agreed. 'An' I been thinkin' on it, Matt, I truly have.'

'So what are we gonna do?' the old man demanded.

'Why, find us a right good place to camp, build a big fire o' green wood and have us a cup o' coffee,' Reilly offered mildly.

'Fire o' green wood . . . why

that'd . . . ' Crane spluttered, then his brain caught up with his mouth and he stopped, eyeing his friend in brooding speculation.

'It ain't gonna work, Fargo,' he stated finally. 'Even Owen ain't that stupid and even if he was, he'll have *hombres* along with him who ain't.'

'Sure,' Reilly admitted, 'I know that. So this is what we're gonna do . . . '

11

'That marshal fella ain't as smart as everybody figgered,' Owen Ducane said to nobody in particular. 'This is a sure enough set-up.'

Dusk had fallen with its characteristic south-western swiftness before Ducane and his men had found the night camp of the men they were following.

On the face of it, Reilly and Crane were showing a lamentable lack of caution.

Two figures lay rolled in their blankets, one on either side of a fire which was sending up a thin streamer of smoke into the clear, crisp night air. As a final homely touch, the figure nearest the watchers had an old black sombrero tipped across his face.

Plainly, it was the sort of camp that was made by men unsuspecting, apparently not ready for trouble and it hadn't fooled Owen Ducane one bit.

'It's a set-up, Garcia,' Ducane repeated, speaking this time to the swarthy Mexican at his side, who had been promoted to the post of Ducane *segundo* on the death of Vicente.

'Of course, *señor*, neither of them was wearing a sombrero like that,' Garcia pointed out. 'The gringos are waiting in the rocks for us to rush the camp. Then they will shoot, kill maybe enough of us to give them a good start.'

'Only we ain't about to oblige them!' Ducane sneered. 'Leave two men we can spare with the horses,' he ordered. 'Have the others leave their rifles and split up into two groups and work along both sides of that clearing. Catch both o' them alive if you can,' he finished, eyes alight with a gleam of anticipation. 'I wanna see those bastards wriggle.'

★ ★ ★

'Well, you called it about right, Fargo,' Crane admitted softly, as he watched

140

the Ducane riders leave their horses in charge of the two who were to remain behind, before the rest made for the clearing with its two blanket-swathed dummies.

'An' I can see why you wanted that hat, but what you figure to do now? It better be right quick,' the old man went on softly, rising behind a solitary stunted cottonwood and dragging his spare blanket off his back, before silently shaking it free of the layer of dirt and dead leaves which had served to camouflage him, ''cause it ain't gonna take them long to find out we ain't where they think we are.'

'Take the guards first,' Reilly ordered, carefully folding his own blanket, 'then we'll figure the rest.'

Silently, the two lawmen moved through the low, scrubby underbrush until they were behind the first of those left behind. Steel fingers closed around the man's throat and a swiftly applied gun butt removed any interest he may have had in subsequent proceedings.

The second man should have been dealt with as noiselessly, but, as luck would have it, Crane stumbled over a root in the darkness, and the guard turned, loosing off a shot before Reilly's rock-hard fist slammed into his jaw.

'Pick us out four good horses, Matt,' Reilly ordered swiftly. busy securing his prisoner. 'Ones we can use to ride relay. Rifles, grub, cartridges. And bring me a rifle up here, will you. We ain't outa this yet.'

'We sure as hell ain't!' Crane agreed vehemently.

★   ★   ★

It was three minutes before the first of the Ducane riders came cautiously through the sparse trees. Reilly waited until the man was within a hundred yards, then drilled him neatly through the thigh. It wasn't humanity that prompted his choice of target: wounded men have to be cared for, at the very least they would have to be returned to the home ranch under escort, depriving Ducane of manpower at a time when he could least afford it.

Having dropped the first man, Reilly moved, having chosen his position so as to be able to do so without exposing himself to those advancing towards him. His wisdom in choosing this course of action was immediately apparent, because, without warning, the log behind which he had been sheltering was suddenly subjected to a hail of bullets. Reilly grinned and shot another Ducane rider carefully through the shoulder.

'Tut, tut,' he murmured quietly, hearing the man's low voiced, monotonous cursing as once again he shifted towards the restive herd of horses. 'He sure ain't gonna get no Sunday-school prize.'

Calmly he waited, aware that time was, for once, on his side, until a low whistle informed him that all was in readiness.

Gathering his feet under him, he inched backwards, when suddenly, there was a hail of bullets from a point a hundred yards to his left.

'*Yeeeehah!*' a cracked old voice bellowed, sending the maddened remnant of the Ducane pony herd dashing madly back up the trail, away from their riders, several trailing branches of mesquite raising clouds of swirling, choking dust to add to the confusion.

'Get the hell on this horse!' the old voice snapped irritably and Reilly found a set of reins shoved into his hand, as he booted home his rifle before hauling himself into the saddle and turning to follow his companion.

★　★　★

'So you figure that followin' these here tracks are gonna bring us up against them guns Ducane's got hid out somewheres?' Crane demanded.

'Perzactly,' Reilly answered shortly, rising from his study of the vague ruts in the trail, which they had been following since escaping the Ducane riders. 'How much start you think we got on them, Matt?' he demanded.

'Half a day to catch up them ponies; they got wounded too,' the old man began judiciously. 'I figure we're a day in front. And we oughta stay there with these fellas, he went on, complacently patting the neck of the chestnut thoroughbred he was riding, which had recently been the property of one Owen Ducane. 'Unless, o' course,' he finished sternly, 'you waste time lookin' at them tracks when you know full well where they're headin'!'

'An' where's that, you ol' buzzard?' Reilly demanded, although he knew the answer well enough.

'Christ, Fargo,' Crane snapped, 'you know as well as I do. We're on the road to Perdition.'

'Well, all I can say is, I sure as hell hope you ain't a true prophet,' Reilly replied sardonically, rising and swinging into the saddle.

★ ★ ★

'Looks peaceful, don't it.' Crane said quizzically, as Reilly studied the little town that had been their destination in the glaring mid-morning light.

'Sure,' Reilly agreed. 'Looks peaceful,' he finished, tendering his battered Army field-glasses. 'Take a look at the jail.'

Both chairs on the shady porch were occupied and, after making a minute adjustment to the instrument's focus, Crane whistled softly.

'What in hell is that fat bastard Bull doin' outa jail?' Crane demanded of no one in particular.'

'Mebbe he figures to run for sheriff,' came the sardonic reply. 'Come on, you ol' fool,' Reilly went on irritably, 'I gotta check somethin'.'

* * *

'What in hell are we doin' here?' Crane demanded, not for the first time, as Reilly peered through one of the stunted mesquite bushes which shielded their refuge.

146

They had waited more or less patiently in their dry, fireless camp under the rim until late afternoon, before making their way down through the rock and scree which bordered the main trail leading down into the little township, where they had found a convenient hollow protected by scant vegetation, overlooking the dusty road.

'There's a lot about this set-up that don't ring true,' Reilly began, turning back to his companion, apparently satisfied with his careful scrutiny of the town. 'Sure, I'm agreeing that Ducane needs somewhere for his men to spend their money and it's got to be somewhere that ain't too particular about law and order,' he went on, 'but this one-horse hole in the wall ain't worth the trouble he's takin' over it. Unless there's some other reason he needs it,' Reilly finished.

'Like what?' Crane asked reasonably.

'Like a store for the guns and ammunition he's shippin' out.'

'No good,' Crane stated immediately.

'He'd have to have them somewheres close to the coast. He can't be movin' guns any sort of distance while the ship's waitin' offshore.'

'That's right,' Reilly admitted, 'but he couldn't store guns, and especially powder and cartridges, anywhere that ain't perfectly dry. I figure that barn in the hills I burned was where he kept the wagons, but the guns and cartridges were somewhere else, somewhere real safe until he was ready to ship them, But — '

'But it's too far to move the stuff in one go, so he uses Perdition as a kinda . . . kinda . . . stagin' post,' Crane supplied.

'That may be more right than you know. Matt,' Reilly agreed thoughtfully. 'I hadn't thought of it before, but they'd sure need somewhere to change and rest the horses.'

'An' don't fergit, that trail is the only pass through them rocks a wagon can use on this stretch o' coast,' Crane added. 'So what now?' the old man went on, casting an eye upwards. 'Be dark in less'n an hour.'

'It's pretty simple,' Reilly explained. 'If they're workin' like I said, they got to have a barn at least as big as the one I found to hide the wagons and guns. There's at least one I know of and that's the place Henry Vance uses for a warehouse. Are there any others?'

'Sure,' Crane admitted, 'a couple that might suit. You want to start now?'

'Nope,' came the drowsy answer from beneath a tipped-forward Stetson, 'I like it good and dark afore I do my sneakin' around.'

★　★　★

Investigation of Vance's warehouse, the first place the pair examined, proved disappointing, the building itself being both too small and too close to the centre of town to be a good candidate for a smuggler's hiding place. They had no more luck with the second building and Crane shook his head dubiously over their final destination.

'It's sure big enough and it's right the hell away from everything, but you know who it belongs to?' the old man demanded.

'Sure,' Reilly nodded, 'but it won't hurt to take a look now, will it?'

Full dark had descended by the time the pair had reached their final destination and, after a quick examination of the surrounding area, Reilly eased open the door of the big wooden barn and slipped inside noiselessly, followed by his companion.

'Looks like we found what we're lookin' for, Matt,' Reilly offered quietly as a single all-embracing glance took in the two heavily loaded ranch wagons and the piles of robust, characteristically shaped wooden boxes occupying every corner of the barn.

'Watch the door,' Reilly ordered quietly, 'while I just make sure we've got what we come for.'

Taking care not to disturb the ropes retaining it, the man from Tucson slid aside the tarpaulin covering the load, to find himself looking down at a heavy wooden crate marked with a collection of letters, made almost indecipherable by an attempt to plane them off. *Almost* indecipherable, but not quite.

For some moments, Reilly mouthed silently by the light of the stable lantern, when a burst of shouting sounded from outside.

'Fargo!' Crane hissed unnecessarily, 'we got company!'

'Give me a hand, quick!' Reilly snapped.

Together, the pair quickly returned the tarpaulin to its original state, with the voices growing nearer every second. The door was actually being pushed open as Reilly repositioned the last fold and snapped, 'Quick! Under the wagon.'

Fortunately, the wagons had originally been designed as the low slung Conestoga type known as a prairie schooner, so, although there was space beneath, the two lawmen were not immediately visible to the newcomers.

This happy situation wasn't set to last, however, because almost immediately a loud authoritative voice snapped, 'Get these goddamn wagons outa here! They gotta be well on their way to the caves before daylight.'

12

'What now?' Crane hissed vehemently, fluidly palming a revolver. 'We could make a run for it.'

'They'd down us sure,' Reilly snapped back, swiftly examining the bottom of the wagon.

'Then I guess there ain't nothin' for it . . . ' Crane began drawing his legs up, preparatory to diving from under the wagon.

'Hold on just a minute, Matt,' Reilly interrupted, in a fierce whisper. 'We ain't dead yet. Give me a hand with this possum belly.'

The possum belly, a square of tough leather used to collect buffalo chips and other inflammable material along the trail, so as to ensure a good fire in the evening, was secured to the frame of the wagon by several large nails.

With desperate strength, Reilly tore

the tough leather loose along part of the back edge. He and Crane had barely managed to wriggle into the narrow pocket so formed, when, with a volley of shouted orders and curses, the wagon lurched forward into the welcoming darkness, with their temporary hiding place creaking ominously.

Suddenly, without warning, the nails holding one side of the hide parted with a rush. Grabbing desperately, Reilly managed to pull himself upwards, while Crane, who still had some support from the leather, gave what little help he could.

Feeling as though his arms where about to tear out of their sockets, Reilly hung on grimly, until, not a second too soon, the wagon lurched to a halt.

'What now?' Crane whispered as, having secured their teams, the voices of its drivers began to fade into the distance.

'Well, I don't know about you,' Reilly replied breathlessly, 'but I ain't figurin' on staying here!'

Suiting the action to the words, the man from Tucson wriggled backwards out of the enfolding leather.

Cautiously, he poked his head from under the wagon, only to find its team still hitched but tied to a convenient post of the nearby corral.

Moments later, he and Crane were erect on the side of the wagon away from the town buildings.

'What in hell are we waitin' for?' the old man snapped. 'Let's get the hell out of here!'

'Now just hold on a second, Matt,' Reilly began thoughtfully, 'we might be able to make somethin' outa this.

'Get back to the livery barn,' Reilly said, after a moment's swift thought. 'Saddle a coupla ponies and bring 'em round just below that ridge. When you see these wagons leaving, follow 'em and, Matt, make sure they don't see you,' he finished with a quick grin.

'I ain't gonna be blowin' no trumpets either, if that's all right with you,' Crane said with some asperity, 'an' while I'm doin' all the work, where in hell are you gonna be?'

'Me?' Reilly said disingenuously. 'Why, I'm gonna be takin' a buggy ride. Get goin'.'

And Crane, sufficiently experienced in the ways of his young friend, promptly got.

Crouched in the shadow of the wheel of the wagon he and Crane had utilized for their escape, Reilly was soon rewarded by the sight of the two wagon drivers approaching their vehicles.

'Stay behind me, Juan, you damned greaser,' the leading figure ordered, moving towards the further wagon. 'I ain't trustin' you away from me in the dark.'

His only answer was a grunt and, as the second man stooped to unhitch his team, Reilly moved, cat-like.

One swift, soundless grab secured the man by the neck and, seconds later, Reilly lowered his senseless victim to the ground. It was the work of moments to secure the man's hands and feet and haul him into the back of the wagon, then Reilly was on the box of the vehicle, reins in hand, turning the team up the trail after his cursing companion, as he gingerly clapped on his victim's greasy sombrero.

'I sure hope that *hombre* don't look back too much come daylight,' Reilly offered doubtfully, shrugging deeper into his victim's foul-smelling buffalo robe.

★ ★ ★

He needn't have worried. It still wanted an hour to dawn when the leading wagon drew to a halt on a level spot beside the trail.

'I ain't goin' down that goddamn slope until daylight,' the leading driver called back. 'I figure to get some sleep an' I don't want to be woke up! You savvy, you goddamn greaser bastard?'

Without waiting for an answer the man pulled a voluminous bedroll from the back of his wagon and dropped it next to the front wheel. Having ground

157

hitched the team to a suitable rock and clumsily rearranged the blankets to his satisfaction, he lay down in the unsavoury mess.

Snores soon assured the interested Reilly that his companion would present no further problem. He dropped lightly from the wagon box, just as a voice behind him asked, 'So what do we do now?'

'That's a real good way to get yourself killed, Matt,' Reilly hissed, slipping away his Colt.

'Huh, I thought you was mebbe expectin' me,' the old man rejoined. 'Your new friends not bein' perzactly sweet-smellin'.'

'It's perzactly the sort o' company I'm gettin' used to,' Reilly retorted, with a grin, 'Get back up the trail, you ol' fool, and watch for company while I do a l'il prospectin'.'

'Bring me back a nugget,' came the sarcastic retort, accompanied by the crisp sound of a Winchester's action being worked.

A swiftly applied gun butt rendered the first driver even more deeply unconscious and Reilly swiftly secured his arms and legs, ensuring that he would be unable to interfere even when he awoke.

'So now,' Reilly told himself, 'I guess we better see what's so all-fired interesting at the bottom of this slope.'

★ ★ ★

The grade wasn't particularly steep or difficult and Reilly was beginning to wonder at his last victim's caution, when he suddenly found himself at the bottom of the slope, with sand covering his boots.

'Yeah, tricky,' Reilly conceded. 'Them *hombres* would need to take it easy, even in daylight and if the harness weren't in good shape and they hit bottom at any sorta speed . . . '

Intrigued by the thought taking shape in his mind, Reilly turned left and began to trudge through the sand, keeping close to the line of cliffs, which soon began to loom above him.

Suddenly, he jerked to a halt before moving swiftly into the deep shadow thrown by the rock next to his right hand. Faint but unmistakable cigarette smoke wafted down the breeze. Somewhere ahead, and not too far at that, someone was enjoying a smoke where no someone ought to be.

'Moonlight in a while,' Reilly told himself cautiously. 'Guess I'll wait till I can see good.'

That proved a sensible precaution, because the fitful light from the waning moon revealed that the cliff he had been following turned sharply right.

Cautiously moving forward, Reilly suddenly found just before this invisible corner, that sand had given way to rock and, moreover, the narrow ledge he had suddenly found himself on had a distinct upward slope.

Carefully, Reilly removed his battered Stetson, before crouching down and inching his way around the corner.

'I thin' the ol' man has got rocks in his head,' a voice said suddenly, seeming to come out of nowhere. 'No one is gonna find this place.'

A foot moved, kicking a rock from the path ahead and, assured of the men's position, Reilly continued his slow advance, as the second voice replied.

'Well, Pedro *amigo*, I sure wish you luck if you're gonna be the one to tell him. The boys an' me'll make sure you get a bang-up funeral,' it finished maliciously.

'You got me wrong,' the first voice protested as, with a final silent movement, Reilly brought the two sentries into his range of vision.

Both men were standing with their backs to him and it was all Reilly could do to suppress a whistle of admiration at the view which stretched out before him.

The rock ledge upon which he lay rose up gently until it was some ten feet above the enveloping sand, extending as it did, for several hundred yards around the cliff.

Opening from this ledge was a series of wide openings in the cliff face, several being tall enough for a man to enter without stooping, while barely a quarter of a mile away, Reilly could make out a rock-bound inlet, which branched into a tiny, natural cove.

Conveniently, the ledge which served the caves in the cliffs terminated in a rock platform within this cove, where Reilly could clearly see coils of rope and the other paraphernalia needed for mooring a substantial ship.

'Anyhow,' the second sentry went on, 'after tonight, we'll be back in Perdition spending our coin — '

'Sure,' his companion interrupted, 'if that goddamn pirate Adams keeps his part of the bargain!'

'Why shouldn't he?' his companion asked reasonably. 'He gets paid on delivery and where is he gonna find another customer who can pay the price the old man's gettin' for those

Gatlings, let alone the rest of what we got in back?

'No,' the second voice went on, 'he'll be here. But, talkin' o' them guns, I wonder where in hell Henderson and that lazy bastard Juan are? Ain't gonna be long before Wes and the rest o' them show up.'

'You know that fat gringo,' the other replied. 'He don' like the trail down in the dark. He's probably sleepin' at the top of the cliff.'

'Be light in a while, I guess we can wait . . . ' The rest of the sentence was lost on Reilly, who had slipped back the way he had come with the beginnings of a desperate plan forming in his mind.

★   ★   ★

'Jesus, Fargo,' Crane began in a barely suppressed whisper, 'I knew you was crazy, but hell, this idea o' yourn has got a dozen ways to get us killed afore we even start!'

Having made his silent way back up

the trail from the beach, Reilly had swiftly located his faithful deputy and laid his plan before him, eliciting much the response he'd expected.

'And anyhow, first you gotta convince that greaser Juan not to talk. How you gonna do that?'

'Wake him up and you'll surely see,' came the complacent response.

★　★　★

'So, if you talk, El Diablo Blanco will send you to the mesquite,' Reilly finished, releasing the petrified man's shirt so that he sprawled in the dust, 'An' you know how Señor Owen treats any who go there?'

Clearly he did, from the way his face blanched and his lip trembled.

'So, *amigo*,' Reilly went on coaxingly, 'just say nothing. After all, what are these gringos to you? And anyway, we, my *compadre* and me, will be on the trail back to town before they can catch us. So, telling your *amigos* would do them no good. And it could be very, very painful for you. *Comprende?*'

A terrified nod was all the answer Reilly needed.

'Give me a hand with these boxes, Matt,' his companion ordered, turning away, apparently satisfied with Juan's answer.

'You figure he'll keep shut, Fargo?' Crane asked curiously.

'Don't matter one way or the other,' came the sardonic reply. 'Oh, and don't forget them cartridges and that manual.'

13

'Sure wish Juan had kept his mouth shut,' Reilly offered.

'I'm bettin' he does too, now,' his companion responded callously, watching a distant Wes Ducane slam his pistol into the side of the unfortunate Juan's head.

Having ridden away from the Mexican and the still unconscious Henderson, apparently carrying out their expressed intention of returning to Perdition, Reilly and Crane had circled rapidly once out of sight of the wagons.

Hidden behind a little rise of ground overlooking the stationary vehicles, the lawmen had been able to observe Henderson's ill-tempered recovery and the subsequent arrival of Wes Ducane and his riders, as well as the violent beating of the unfortunate Mexican.

Apparently satisfied that Juan had

nothing more to say, Ducane turned away from his victim and issued a series of rapid orders, which sent half his force scurrying to their mounts and riding off in the direction taken by Reilly and his companion.

'Bad tactics, splittin' your force in the face o' the enemy,' Reilly stated easily. 'Two hours to sundown,' he went on, settling his Stetson over his face. 'Did you cut them traces like I told you?' he demanded unnecessarily.

'Sure did,' Crane chuckled, lined brown face creasing into an unaccustomed grin. 'Ain't you gonna stay awake an' see the fun?'

'Nope,' came the drowsy answer, 'I got a long night ahead. An' you better hope no one counts them boxes!'

*　*　*

'Get them wagons movin'.' Wes Ducane had had enough of problems for the day. The wagons containing what his father always referred to as 'special merchandise' still had to be brought to the bottom of the slope and their contents manhandled across the beach. And it had to be done with much less than an hour of daylight left.

'What in hell are you waitin' for, Henderson?' he demanded, as the teamster skilfully eased the big freight wagon onto the shallow grade.

'If'n you want this stuff at the bottom in one piece, you best leave me do it my way!' the other retorted. ''Less'n you wanna handle these here ribbons yourself!'

Receiving no response but an ill-disposed glare, the fat man returned his attention to his team, carefully easing them forward and on to the long rocky slope to the beach.

Feeling the vehicle's rear wheels grind on to the beginnings of the grade, Henderson eased the reins back carefully, throwing the full weight of wagon on to the harness, thus allowing him to control the descent by utilizng the strength of his team and without unnecessary use of the brake.

Seeing this first wagon safely started, Ducane signalled impatiently to Juan, who moved his wagon forward nervously.

Copying Henderson's actions almost exactly, the Mexican had barely drawn his wagon on to the top of the slope when there was a crack like the report of a pistol and the second wagon slammed into the hind legs of its instantly terrified team, pushing them aside and hurtling down the slope to collide with Henderson's vehicle.

Unable to halt this headlong flight, both horses and vehicles drove into the sand at the bottom of the rock slope, the wagons bouncing off their wheels to roll over and over in the sand, harness and wagon tongues having broken almost simultaneously, to leave the terrified animals, on their feet and badly shaken but apparently otherwise unscathed.

'Jesus H. Christ,' Wes Ducane swore violently, leading the way down the slope at a run and sliding to a halt next to the inert body of Juan.

'Cashed,' one of his men exclaimed, kneeling to examine the Mexican. 'Neck's broke,' he added unnecessarily. 'Wonder where at's Henderson?'

'In hell, I hope,' Ducane snarled, 'an' if he ain't, he's gonna wish hisself there by the time I finish with the bastard.'

* * *

Twilight had already fallen with its characteristic desert swiftness, when Crane heard a low whisper from the figure next to him.

'How'd it work, Matt?' Reilly asked, all trace of sleep gone from his voice.

'Sweet,' Crane answered shortly, the darkness hiding his grin. 'They took Juan out of the wreck, plumb dead, but his *compadre*, the other driver, was makin' more'n enough noise to make up for it.'

'Where's he at?' Reilly demanded, slipping into the greasy sombrero and foul buffalo coat of the late and unlamented Juan.

'Back aways,' Crane responded. 'They moved him clear of the wagons and ol' Wes's had 'em clearin' the stuff ever since. Sounds like they still got a fair ways to go, though,' he added helpfully.

'I'd best be movin' then,' Reilly murmured. 'Don't forget, soon as the shootin' starts, get them ponies to the bottom o' the slope. I'll be in a hurry and won't have time for no society gossip! And don't forget them pack ponies!' Then he was gone before his companion could offer any further comment.

Ducane and his men had no time to spare from the job in hand to notice a single further addition to their working party and carrying a wooden box labelled cartridges proved sufficient disguise to allow Reilly access to the first of the large store caves.

Given the nature of the material stored here, work was being sensibly conducted by the fitful light of a fire lit well away from the entrance and Reilly had no trouble in depositing his box and then slipping aside between the rows of packing cases.

Here, however, his luck ran out. Case after case revealed only rifles and a few pistols, many of them having seen hard use.

The contents of one case, however, drew a long whistle from the revolver expert.

'Now if that ain't some sort o' equalizer,' Reilly muttered, hefting the big Le Mat revolver he had found from the packing case.

'Nine chambers and a nice shotgun barrel underneath,' he informed himself, rummaging briskly and drawing a second, similar weapon into the light. Brand new and chambered for .44 cartridges, too! Sure feels like Christmas. I'm guessin' Matt won't mind me playin' Santa Claus.'

Shoving his new acquisitions into his belt, Reilly shouldered his disguise and moved quickly out of this first cave and into its neighbour.

This time his luck was in.

Gunpowder, in twenty-pound barrels, was stacked around the walls, while cartridges boxes, similar to the one Reilly was carrying, were carefully layered in front of them. Space, however, had been left between the boxes so as to allow the barrels to be moved first.

Clearly, someone had given thought to the loading requirements of the vessels used to transport this sort of dangerous cargo. Which suited the Marshal of Perdition very well.

Working slowly, Reilly carefully lowered his burden to the ground and straightened up. Momentarily finding himself alone in the fitful light of the cave, he immediately slipped between some nearby boxes.

Swift and silent, Reilly quickly appropriated a fresh supply of cartridges for his own weapons, as well as those of his partner.

'Now where in hell do these boys keep their slow match?' Reilly demanded, carefully scanning the walls as he stuffed cartridges into his new, nine-chambered revolver. Thorough investigation didn't help and Reilly swore disgustedly under his breath.

'Guess it'll have to be a powder trail,' he told himself dubiously, 'though I sure as hell don't like the idea o' settin' it off. And how in hell am I gonna lay it with these son of bitches in and out of the cave all the time?'

Almost on the heels of that thought, there came a stentorian bellow, apparently from the mouth of the cave, which sent Reilly's hand streaking to his pistol.

This first alarm was soon followed by several others and a rush of boots along the adjoining ledge. Peering out of the cave mouth, Reilly quickly saw the source of all the excitement.

A dainty fore and aft rigged clipper, speed inherent in her every line, was being cautiously worked into the little cove and the whole gang were quickly making their way down to the tiny, rock-hewn jetty to greet what seemed like friends and compatriots.

'Too good to miss,' Reilly told himself, as he turned away and began cautiously to remove the lid from one of the twenty-pound barrels.

Ten minutes later, he carefully set down the barrel which he had used to lay his powder trail and fumbled in a pocket, withdrawing a candle stub he had found in the back of the cave and an old lantern which still contained a splash of kerosene.

Working precisely, Reilly cut a hole near the bottom of the candle, right through from side to side. Next he removed his worn old bandanna, twirling the ends between his fingers to form a short rope, before soaking the makeshift fuse so formed in his meagre supply of kerosene.

It was the work of moments to push the kerosene soaked bandanna through the hole in the bottom of the candle and then stand the candle upright near the rock wall, with its attached fuse trailing neatly into a pile of gunpowder surrounding the whole device.

Finally satisfied with his arrangements, Reilly took a deep breath and scratched a match.

Holding the flame at arm's length, he lit the candle before gingerly lowering the now empty gunpowder barrel over his detonator. A sliver of rock under the barrel's rim allowed free access to the flaming powder trail. Reilly breathed a sigh of relief as a glance through the knothole he had previously knocked out of one of the barrel's staves, showed the candle alight and burning healthily.

Straightening heavily from his home-made detonator, he moved towards the cave's opening where a quick glance showed most of the gang were still occupied with mooring the ship.

'Hmm,' Reilly pondered, scrubbing thoughtfully at a bristly chin, while settling his stolen sombrero more firmly over his face. 'Ain't never blowed up a ship afore. Wonder just how you might go about it? Guess the first thing to do is get aboard.'

This proved easier than Reilly might have expected. Frequent comings and goings across the gang plank allowed him to slip aboard as part of a group moving cargo. Some of Ducane's men had plainly been making free with the ship's liquor store and amid the red faces and increasingly raucous laughter, Reilly slipped unnoticed down a companionway.

At the bottom of the narrow, railed stairway he found himself faced with several passages, one leading aft, towards what was plainly the officers' accommodation, while the other two led forward, one terminating in a flight of rough steps.

Choosing this latter, Reilly soon found himself in bowels of the vessel. Luck came his way again because the first door he tried proved to be the tiny powder magazine.

Here, supplies of both slow and quick

match meant the construction of a fuse was simplicity itself and having made a rapid calculation, Reilly cut his fuse for thirty minutes, giving, he hoped, ample time for a leisurely escape.

Moments later, he was in the passageway, gently closing the door of the magazine and then making his way silently up the rough stairway which led to deck.

At the bottom of the stairs leading to the deck he halted, listening. A quick glance showed no one in sight and coming to a rapid decision. Reilly slipped along the passageway leading to the officers' accommodation.

The first three doors he tried each led into the sort of tiny cubby-hole that was clearly designed for junior crew members, but the next door, letting into a cabin built across the stern of the vessel, looked more promising.

Both fittings and furnishings were of good quality, including a large desk which immediately became the focus of Reilly's attention. Its drawers yielded quickly to an expertly used paper knife and Reilly had just begun his study of an absorbing sheaf of papers, which included several of the vessel's bills of lading, when the sound of raised voices preceded the rattle of the cabin's door knob.

14

Like lightning, Reilly bundled the papers into his shirt and snatching out a Colt, slipped into the leg well of the desk.

It was not a moment too soon because he had barely time to settle himself before the voices rose in volume and he recognized Wes Ducane's nasal whine.

'I can't figure where the hell that Gatling's gone,' Ducane complained wearily.

'Perhaps the old man made a mistake and miscounted,' said a deeper, colder voice, larded with disbelief. 'Anyhow,' this individual went on, ignoring Ducane's contemptuous snort, 'I ain't paying for what I ain't got.' There was a rapid rustling of bills, then the voice went on, 'I guess you'll find that correct.'

The rustling was repeated, then Ducane snarled, 'This is a thousand short!'

'Call it *inconvenience money*,' the other snapped. 'Now get out and tell your pa, next time a shipment's short, I won't want any of it!'

Boots scuffed across the wooden floor, and a door slammed, signalling Ducane's departure. Glass clinked against glass, then there was a splash of liquid and a second pair of boots, heavier than the first, thudded across the floor towards the desk.

Reilly saw blue serge-clad legs move round the desk, topped by a thickset body and a hard, bloated face.

Shock flashed across the seaman's face as his eyes met Reilly's and his gun hand leapt pocket-wards, the glass it had previously held dropping to the floor. The hand froze instantly as Reilly jerked the barrel of his revolver significantly, enjoining and obtaining instant obedience.

'Back up,' came the terse order and,

reluctantly, the man complied, coming to a halt by the ledge surrounding the stern windows and perching himself there.

'Give me that oilskin,' Reilly ordered, exiting his hiding place and indicating a sheet of that material which had been dropped in the corner of the room.

As the big man turned to obey, Reilly took one long step and smashed the butt of his pistol into the side of his head.

The officer sprawled, barely stunned, and Reilly struck again, this time dropping the man unconscious.

'You're gonna have to take your chance, *amigo*,' Reilly said, wrapping his sheaf of papers into a neat package, surrounded by oilskin and tied with a piece of tarred string which he appropriated from his victim's pocket. A second string secured the two Le Mats to Reilly's body, and his Colts were thrust deeply into their holsters and secured as the man from Tucson stepped quickly to the window and swung his legs over the sill.

Before he could slip off into the water, however, his world erupted into a volcano of fire and smoke.

The magazine had gone off early.

Reilly came back to consciousness, moments later, with the coppery taste and smell of blood in his mouth and nose. He found himself in the water, floating away from the stricken vessel, now lying with half its stern blown off.

Desperately, he turned over and struck out for a nearby piece of wreckage, which, luckily, seemed substantial enough to support him.

Throwing his arm across this timely support, Reilly found that, with the tide now fortunately on the rise, he was being carried back towards the beach. And, as if to set the finish on the night's proceedings, suddenly the caves to shoreward were lit by a second blinding flash, followed by a thunderous roar, signalling the perfect operation of Reilly's first makeshift detonator.

★ ★ ★

'Jesus, boy.' Crane's voice sounded softly out of the darkness as Reilly's feet touched ground and he fought desperately against the cold which seemed to permeate his whole body.

'Hold on, son,' the voice sounded again, closer, as a substantial, muscular arm slipped under his shoulders and lifted him bodily clear of the water.

'We gotta move, Fargo,' Crane spoke anxiously. 'Can you ride?'

'S-s-sure,' Reilly shivered, levering himself upright and all but falling across the saddle of the pony Crane had directed him to.

A gentle whicker greeted his arrival and a velvet nose pushed towards the pocket of his jeans, as the pony stood rocklike without so much as an ear flick.

'Pecos, goddamn it, you ol' crowbait, what in hell you doin' here?' Reilly blurted, shock and a wave of gladness jerking him out of his half swoon.

'Figured you'd want him,' Crane observed complacently, 'only don't ever ask me to saddle the l'il bastard again,' the old gunman snapped, returning to irascibility on the instant. 'Goddamn l'il goat tried to take my arm off!'

'Glad he didn't,' Reilly returned with a worn grin, tiredly shoving the oilskin-wrapped package into a convenient saddle-bag. 'I don't want him gettin' blood poisonin'. Let's ride!' he finished, before Crane could frame a suitable reply. 'We got business . . . '

* * *

'Present for you, Matt,' Reilly said absently, as he felt in the backstrap of his jeans to drag out the second Le Mat, now sadly waterlogged. 'She may need cleanin' up afore you can use 'er,' he added with a grin, as he took his own belt from Pecos's saddle and strapped it on, having finished restoring his own Colts and Le Mat to working order.

An all night ride had brought the two lawmen to their refuge near the town and Reilly had used the few minutes before dawn to return himself and his equipment to its normal condition.

Leaving Crane contentedly working on his new pistol, Reilly crept to the top of the little rise behind which they had sheltered the ponies and the pack-horses bearing Ducane's *special merchandise*.

Carefully, he edged above the ridge and looked across the intervening distance towards the little town at the centre of all the preceding violence.

'Sure looks peaceful,' Reilly told himself, taking in the absence of sentries and overall air of indolence which pervaded the place, as he absently reached into a hidden pocket in his vest and pulled out the battered object it contained.

'Federal business now, then?' Crane offered, seeing the scuffed Deputy Federal Marshal's badge pinned to Reilly's equally dilapidated calfskin vest. 'You know you ain' got a smidgen' o' jurisdiction down here, don't you?'

'They got a right to know who's takin' them back to hang,' came the hard reply. 'You ready?'

'Nope,' came the equally caustic response, 'but let's do 'er anyways.'

★ ★ ★

'You sure them greasers are doing their job properly, Bull?' Stark Ducane demanded nervously, for the tenth time in as many minutes, as he tossed back his drink.

'If'n you ain't satisfied,' the big man rumbled, before also throwing a slug of liquor down his capacious gullet, 'whyn't you go round and check 'em yourself? An' if'n you ain't gonna do that, shut the hell up!'

'You ain't got no right to talk to me that way!' his younger, smaller brother whined. 'Hell, Bull, you an' me, we oughta be helpin' each other, not arguing. I got something here,' he went on, patting the fat Morocco-bound account book which he had not once put down since arriving in the township earlier in the day, 'which could make both of us rich.'

He glanced across the hard-packed dirt floor of the cantina in which they were sitting, to where Perdition's entire male population sat under the guns of three of Ducane's Mexican *vaqueros*.

'This book,' he went on, dropping his voice conspiratorially, 'is worth millions . . . millions, I tell you!'

'Sure, Stark, sure,' his brother began placatingly, 'millions, you already told me a coupla times. But you never said why.'

'It's a list of everything the old man ever did and everyone he ever paid off, every name, every address. His whole organization,' Stark began. 'With this,' he went on, 'we can just carry on where the old fool left off! But without it . . . we'd have been nowhere.'

'Seems to me it ain't the sort o' thing you should just be wandering around with, Stark,' Bull began uneasily, before continuing, with a worried frown, 'Does Rosa know you've got it with you?'

'That goddamn bitch!' his brother snarled. 'No, she don't know! And I'll tell you somethin' else! If I have anything to do with it, she won't never get anywhere near it!'

'Tryin' to cut us out,' he slurred, the liquor clearly beginning to have its effect. 'She's a hog, wants it all!'

'Guess I'd better check them sentries,' his brother offered dubiously, reaching for his hat as Stark waved a limp hand in acknowledgement. 'Be real careful with that book, l'il brother,' Bull finished almost affectionately, as Stark slumped face down on the table. 'We wouldn't want nothin' to happen to it, now would we?'

★   ★   ★

Outside the cantina, Bull paused, allowing the balmy southern evening to clear, at least partially, some of the whiskey fumes from his head. Slightly refreshed, he settled his battered Stetson more firmly on his frowzy, unkempt hair and stepped off the warped boards of the sidewalk, sauntering sluggishly through the dusty street to where the first of his sentries was keeping watch, probably in company with a bottle.

Behind him a figure moved out of the deeper shadow of the building opposite the little cantina and slipped, catlike, in Bull Ducane's wake.

A short walk brought Ducane to the edge of the corral where his rider was supposed to be watching the ponies.

What he saw as he approached, inflamed his always uncertain temper, although it didn't much surprise him.

His erstwhile sentry was slumped against a post of the corral, in which the pony herd were milling nervously, a half-empty bottle in his left fist, while the right lay concealed behind him. His wide-brimmed sombrero was pushed forward, shielding his face, and his rifle was propped against another post, some distance away.

With a snarl of rage, Ducane reached down to grasp the man's shirt front prior to jerking him to his feet, only to freeze with a look of ludicrous amazement on his face, as a gun barrel stabbed him in the ribs.

'Silence, some folk say, is golden, *amigo*,' an icy voice said satirically in his ear, 'noise, for you, will be leaden, savvy?'

'Get his guns, Matt,' the slumped figure snapped, although his companion was already at work.

'What are we gonna do with this, Fargo?' Crane demanded. 'Personally, I favour shootin' the bastard.'

'You wouldn't do that,' Ducane sneered, although there was a tremor in his voice that made Reilly grin maliciously. 'That'd be murder . . . '

'Your yeller dog of a brother cut up the Apache boy who rode with us like he was a piece of wolf bait,' Reilly snarled, rising in one fluid movement and pushing the barrel of the big Le Mat against the big man's stomach.

'Now, you may not know it, but this here piece has got a shotgun barrel under the one that shoots pistol bullets,' the lawman went on, in a vicious snarl, 'and I just might be inclined to let go this load of buckshot into your yeller guts, just so's we can see how you wriggle, you fat bastard!'

'Aw, don't do that. Fargo,' Crane interrupted. 'You promised me I could shoot 'im,' the old gunfighter went on, coming to stand behind their prisoner and jabbing the barrel of his Remington into Ducane's back just above the belt.

'Ever see anyone die o' being shot in the kidney, Bully boy?' Crane asked sneeringly. 'I figure it'd hafta hurt like hell,' he went on, jabbing with the pistol once again.

'You can't do this,' Ducane replied, but the disbelief was clearly causing his voice to shake. 'You're Federal law.'

'Well that might be true,' Reilly admitted, 'But if'n I ain't lookin' that particular way . . . ' Crane's cackle interrupting him.

'Jesus,' Ducane whined, suddenly finding his not considerable courage running out on him, 'keep that old bastard away from me!'

'Why should I?' Reilly demanded, more for something to say than because he expected any response.

'C-c-cause I got something you need to know,' Ducane whimpered, trying to edge away from an insanely grinning Matt Crane. 'Something important. A-a-about Stark . . . he's got the old man's book . . . '

15

'Easy all!' a hard voice ordered from the doorway of Perdition's cantina, 'Just set right still and no one'll get hurt,' the voice went on, as its owner propelled Bull Ducane through the door to land sprawling at his brother's feet.

'Just set right still,' Reilly repeated his warning, as he eased fluidly through the door, behind a pair of worn Colts.

Moving swiftly past him, Crane stopped midway to the bar, hand hovering over the hammer of his old revolver, allowing Reilly to dominate the situation while still keeping the three Mexicans comfortably under his gun.

'Wha . . . ' Stark began, staring uncomprehendingly at his giant brother cowering on the floor.

Blankly, he shifted his gaze, shock biting into him as he identified the figure in the doorway.

'But how,' Stark went on, rising and slipping his right hand behind the thick book which he still held clasped across his thin chest, 'Wes sent word that you was dead, or as good as . . . '

'You might say,' Reilly offered whimsically, although the pistols grasped in his capable hands wavered not a hair, ' "reports of my death have been greatly exaggerated." I'll take the book,' he finished, lifting his pistols to emphasize the order.

'Like hell!' Stark Ducane returned, snatching his hand from behind the book — only the hand contained a derringer pistol and Ducane's first shot tore Reilly's Stetson from his head as the man from Tucson desperately threw himself sideways, triggering his Colts as he did so.

Caught in the chest by the heavy bullets, Stark was thrown backwards, reflexively triggering the second barrel of his deadly little hideout and driving the bullet into his brother's chest as

Bull came up from the floor. The big man collapsed without a sound and Reilly twisted fast, snapping two slugs into the last remaining Mexican, Crane having despatched the first two with a neat right and left from the worn Remington still dangling from his limp wrist.

Something about the old man's attitude drew Reilly swiftly to his feet, sending him anxiously across the room, to where Crane leant wearily against the bar.

'Matt,' Reilly asked, concern edging his voice, 'are you hit?'

'Last one creased my leg,' the old man admitted with a weak smile, easing away from the bar to show where the blood was welling through the cloth of his jeans from a deep furrow torn in the flesh. 'It ain't much, but I reckon it kinda threw me, Fargo. Hell, I'm sure gettin' too old for this,' he admitted tiredly.

'You an' me both, you worthless ol' goat,' Reilly replied. 'Get that scratch tied up, then get the horses. We ain't outa this yet, not by a damn sight. An' don't get no ideas about loafin' neither. We got work to do.'

'Goddamn it,' Crane snarled, instantly shaken out of his self-pity. 'What in hell does a fella have to do around here to get some rest? We ain't slept in two nights!'

'Plenty o' time for restin' when you're cashed; now, we got business,' Reilly returned, shoving cartridges into the second of his battered Colts before snapping shut the loading gate and making for the door.

'And just where in hell are you going?' Crane demanded, pulling tight the last knot of his makeshift bandage and gingerly setting his foot to the floor.

'To see our esteemed *alcalde*. I'm callin' a town meetin',' his companion retorted, 'and I sure aim to see she's there. Try not to bleed to death 'til I get back.'

★　★　★

'So that's how I figure it,' Reilly finished, turning from his makeshift diagram to address the entire population of Perdition, now crowded into the little cantina, early the next morning. 'They ain't gonna be expectin' us to show fight, so all we gotta do is barricade one end of main street and then wait for them to ride in and be shot.'

'Looks too simple to me,' Henry Vance, the storekeeper, offered dubiously, but before he could go on, Crane, previously primed by Reilly, said, 'But suppose, just suppose, they don't fall for that and come in at the other end of town?'

'They won't,' said Reilly, with an air of arrogant assurance, quite alien to his nature, 'they ain't that smart.'

*   *   *

Black night had long since fallen and the Mexican designated to be messenger of the town's downfall, looked down

198

at his employer.

'Don't worry,' he offered, 'your family will come.'

'I don't care about them,' came the viciously snarled reply. 'Just tell that bitch Rosa; come in from the other end of town and kill them all! All of them, you understand? But especially the marshal and his old fool of a deputy! Now ride!'

'You was right, Fargo,' Crane stated simply, drawing back into the cover of the big livery barn from where the two lawmen had watched the activities of the Mexican and his employer.

'Yeah,' Reilly admitted shortly.

'Get Vance and tell him about the change of plan, then bring them crates around to his warehouse and start unpackin' them. And don't lose none of the parts,' Reilly finished shortly, before turning away. Crane limped after him, wondering at the note of sadness in his companion's voice.

★   ★   ★

'Guess that just about does it, Matt,' Reilly offered, stifling a yawn before reaching up to scrub at gritty, red-rimmed eyes.

'Sure,' the old man agreed, flipping the cover over the object they had been working on for most of the night.

'Be light in a coupla hours,' the older man suggested. 'Henry and the boys are just about set; why don't you turn in? Tomorrow's liable to be a big day.'

'I'd sure like to,' Reilly admitted, 'but I got a hunch I better keep an eye on Mr Ducane's side partner. We don't want nothin to spoil the surprise now, do we?'

It still wanted an hour before dawn when the door of the little house Reilly had been patiently watching, silently opened and a slim, black-dressed figure slipped briskly through and made for the enormous horse barn which adjoined the property.

Saddling swiftly, the figure grasped the reins and turned the little mustang, prior to leading her mount from the stable, when Reilly appeared in the doorway.

''Morning, Miz Wex,' he greeted the black-dressed *alcalde*. 'Kinda early for ridin', ain't it?'

'I-I . . . didn't . . . I mean,' she began, but Reilly forestalled her.

'You better come this way, ma'am,' he interrupted levelly, 'there's a coupla things you might wanta see.'

★ ★ ★

'You knew, didn't you?' Lauren Wex said simply, now standing in the middle of Perdition's main street and inspecting the defences around her. It wasn't even a question.

'Yeah,' Reilly admitted, 'I figured it was a pretty good bet.'

'How did you work it out?' she demanded, 'I thought I'd been pretty clever.'

'You were,' Reilly assured her, 'but I got suspicious right from the start. This town's mostly Mexican and what

201

self-respectin' Mexican man is gonna let a woman run things? Especially a gringo woman?

'Naw, it just didn't fit,' Reilly went on, 'and then when we found them wagon tracks I'd seen in Dragon Wells leadin' into your barn, well, couldn't be no other answer. They needed to keep the guns here before takin' them down to the coast, didn't they?'

'Sure, the old man figured the salt air'd rust them before they could be shipped if we left them in the caves too long. And being the *alcalde* was a good cover. No one would come poking in Miz Wex's barn,' the woman explained simply. 'What happens now? You won't keep them out, you know that, don't you?'

'Gonna have to lock you up,' Reilly replied. 'And I ain't aimin' to keep them out. We mebbe got a few things lined up for your *compadres* that's gonna surprise the hell outa them. And I sure wouldn't want anyone to spoil the party,' he finished sardonically.'

'They aren't my *compadres*, as you

so delicately put it, Mr Reilly, they're my family. At least by marriage. My husband was Bobby, Ducane's eldest son.

'He was going to quit them, go straight; we were going to have a life together and a family,' she went on, as though reciting a litany which she had learned by heart, 'but he got shot in a poker game in Denver. I had no family myself, so I came here with our son. But the old man took the boy and I had to help with their plans or the old man threatened . . . to . . . to — ' she finished incoherently.

'Aw right, Miz Lauren,' Crane, who had been an interested bystander, interrupted. 'I guess you better come along with me. The jail ain't so bad, beds are clean . . . ' His voice tailed off into the distance and Reilly turned back to make yet another round of the town's defences in the slowly welling light, perfectly aware that even a tiny detail overlooked could result in catastrophe.

* ★ ★

'Miz Lauren, I'm sure sorry about this,' Crane began apologetically, ushering the woman into the largest of the jail's two cells, before closing and carefully locking the door, as Lauren Wex seated herself on the bed, demurely crossing her legs beneath her neat riding skirt.

'Now, Señora Gomez here is gonna take care of you, ma'am,' he went on, tendering the keys to the plump, comfortable-looking Mexican woman who stood watchfully behind him.

'She don't come out, *señora*,' Crane instructed, speaking rapidly in Spanish, 'an' unless she's about to die, don't you go in with her.'

'I am not afraid, Señor Crane,' the woman answered stoutly. 'After all, what can she do? She has no weapon.'

Left to herself, Lauren Wex climbed carefully to the barred window of her cell. Her view was, of necessity, restricted but her ears told her all that was required. The town was planning a lethal reception for the hated Ducanes and if the gang followed the instructions she had sent by Phillipe, they would ride to their ultimate destruction. Even if any members escaped, it would do them no good, she conceded. Reilly was clearly a man who finished any job he started.

Carefully, she lowered herself back to the clean swept dirt floor of the cell and returned to her seat on the hard, blanket-covered bunk.

For several minutes she sat motionless, until suddenly from the edge of town there came a piercing shout.

It was too far away for her to hear the words but its signal was rapidly taken up,

'They're coming! It's the Ducanes! Get your guns!'

Lauren Wex waited until the uproar appeared to be at its height, then she hurled herself to the floor, screaming and to all intents and purposes in the throes of a dangerous fit.

Señora Gomez, hearing the noise and

doubtfully approaching the cell door, relaxed slightly.

Her instructions from Señor Crane had been clear, but the gringo woman certainly appeared very sick, if not actually dying.

Reluctantly, Graciella Gomez inserted the big key into the lock and carefully opened the cell door.

Still the woman continued to writhe in pain and now, convinced beyond her better judgement, the Mexican woman reached out a sympathetic hand.

'Señora Wex,' she began, touching the *alcalde*'s flushed face, 'it is I, Graciella Gomez. Are you sick, *señora* . . . ?'

16

Meanwhile, well out of rifle shot of the makeshift barricade erected across the main street, Wes Ducane sat his big sorrel stallion. Carelessly, he surveyed the defences arrayed against him and the thirty or so riders at his back, as the sun made its way above the horizon.

'This is gonna be pie like mother made,' his brother Owen, slightly behind him, said disparagingly. 'All we gotta do is ride down there an' take them,' his younger brother went on, sawing ruthlessly at the mouth of his restless horse and drawing one of his fancy, silver-mounted Colts.

On the face of it, Owen was right. But the man who had blown up Adam's ship and those store caves hadn't seemed, at least to Wes Ducane, like a man to overlook any bets. But there didn't appear to be any real argument about it.

The barricade was exactly where Lauren Wex's messenger had said it would be and there were clearly men moving behind it. Casting aside his doubts, Wes Ducane raised a gloved fist.

'Let's go,' he screamed, suiting the action to the words and sending his big horse forward in a sweeping turn that would take them past the barricade, still well out of rifle range, to circle the town and take its pitiful defenders in the rear, from where Ducane and his riders would then be able to start the massacre.

Past the collection of clapboard and adobe buildings that formed one side of Main Street, the cavalcade thundered and still not a shot was fired in the town's defence. Turning abruptly, Wes Ducane wheeled his column into the far end of the town's main thorough-fare, every man with his weapon cocked, straining for first sight of the easy targets they were all expecting.

Except, of townsfolk, of anything living in fact, there was not a sign.

Confused by this unexpected turn of

events, Ducane led his men at a gallop along dusty Main Street, finding, to his surprise, that every alley, every passageway which might have been wide enough to accommodate a horseman was blocked, shoulder high.

'Whoa,' Ducane roared, raising his hand as the group approached the barricade they had first seen from a distance outside of town.

'W-w-what in hell?' he began, surprise blurring his voice, because over the tongue of one of the wagons forming the barrier stepped a man, wearing two guns and the badge of a United States Deputy Federal Marshal.

'Throw up your hands, boys,' Reilly ordered evenly, 'you're all under arrest.'

For an instant, his very audacity seemed as though it might elicit obedience, but then with a half-mad snarl of rage, Owen Ducane lifted his pistol and drove a bullet at the lounging figure.

But Reilly wasn't there and in an immediate echo of Ducane's shot, there came a murderous, flailing hail of lead from the rooftops and nearby windows, emptying saddles and causing Wes Ducane to snatch his panic-stricken mount rearing back on its hindquarters, whilst screaming, 'Back! Get back up the goddamn street!'

So, not as dumb as that Wex bitch thought, Wes conceded, driving his big stallion into a gallop. But not that smart, either.

'Ain't no way him and his bunch o' storekeepers can keep us from breaking out,' Ducane told himself, 'and then we'll see. Yes, sir, then we'll see.'

He was a bare fifty yards from the end of the street when he saw the familiar multi-barrelled shape and heard the first coffee-mill chatter of the Gatling gun.

'So that's where . . . ' was his last thought on earth as the heavy slugs tore through his chest and his blood spattered the ground below.

★　★　★

'Get 'em all?' Reilly asked, callously.

'You better come see,' Crane growled, wiping a smear of grease from his powder-blackened face, 'and afore you ask, somehow I missed that l'il bastard Owen.'

Sprawled across the dirt floor of the cell, Graciella Gomez was sadly lacking any of the comfortable dignity she had exhibited in life.

Her glazing eyes stared placidly back at Reilly as he swiftly examined the body.

'Knife in the throat, stiletto most likely,' he stated flatly, as he rose to his feet. 'I'm guessin' you never thought to search Miz Wex.'

'Nope,' Crane admitted evenly, 'I couldn't myself and I didn't want to trust poor l'il Graciella in reach of her. So I told her not to go into the cell or near her. Best I could do at the time,' he finished with a shrug.

'Guess so,' Reilly admitted. 'We sure had enough to think of and you're right, you sure couldn't have searched her yourself.'

'Where d'you think she's headin'?' Crane asked.

'Where would you go?' Reilly asked mildly. 'Looks like all our rats are gonna get caught in one trap. You stay and clean house,' he ordered, clicking open the loading gate of his battered Colt, before beginning to push cartridges into the cylinder. 'It's gotta be done right, Matt,' he went on, forestalling his old deputy's protest, 'and with that leg, you can't ride either fast enough or far enough.'

'So where in hell are you goin'?' Crane demanded, 'as if I didn't know.'

'I got a score to pay off,' came the mild reply.

★　★　★

It had been pure luck that Owen had survived the murderous onslaught which had accounted for his older brother and most of their accompanying riders.

Unused to gunfire, his poorly trained and uncooperative horse had shied and skittered uncontrollably until he had managed to get it turned and headed up the street, almost the last of the bunch, with his mount veering towards the edge of the street.

So it was that the first murderous blast of the Gatling which cut down the nearest riders, miraculously missed him, although, by sheer bad luck, a stray bullet had killed his horse.

Almost out of his mind with fear, he had blundered into the nearest alley-way, forced his way past the barrier there and by what seemed like another miracle, had all but run into a straying pony, saddled and riderless.

He had pushed his sorry mount as hard as he dared on the way back to the ranch and it was with a feeling of intense relief that he topped the last rise to sit his badly blown pony, looking down at the main house and its adjacent horse corrals.

★　★　★

'*Rosa, Rosa*!' Owen Ducane began bellowing as soon as he entered the main house, leaving his mount untended by the hitching rail.

'Christ, Owen, you scroungy l'il bastard,' the girl snapped, coming into the corridor from the house's main room, with one of her father's big account books cradled in her hands, 'what in hell's the matter?'

'Everything,' her brother blurted, wide-eyed with fear.

'They trapped us, Sis, killed every man. That damn marshal got hold of one of Pa's Gatlings and when we rode in . . . them bastard storekeepers killed everybody . . . everybody!'

His voice had been pitching higher and higher. bordering on hysteria, and without hesitation, Rosa slapped him hard across the face.

Eyes wide with shock, Owen's hand was dropping towards his pistol when he found himself looking down the barrel of a derringer which had somehow miraculously appeared in his sister's hand.

'Don't make that mistake again,' Rosa gritted. 'You ever try and pull on me, you little bastard, and you'll be in Hell before you touch your gun. Now, tell it to me again, slowly.'

*   *   *

' . . . and you can bet your life that the next place they'll head will be here!' Owen finished, still barely in control of his fear.

'How many men've we got on the damn place now?' his sister snapped, striding to the main door and looking out at the empty horse corral. Not a single animal remained except the worn-out pony which had brought Owen Ducane from Perdition.

'What the . . . ?' the woman began, 'What in hell made them light out like that?'

'Mebbe I can help you there,' a cultured female voice suggested from the corner of the house.

'I told them that Señor Reilly is a

215

deputy federal marshal and that he's on his way out here with a posse, to arrest you and anyone else he finds with you,' Lauren Wex went on, still hidden by the corner of the building. 'They seem to have found discretion the better part of valour, because, last I saw of them, they were riding south, just as fast as they could go!' she finished.

'Christ, you stupid bitch . . . ' Owen began, starting forward with his hand on his single remaining pistol.

'Shut up, Owen,' his sister ordered and her brother subsided, fuming, as Rosa went on. 'You and I have never liked each other, but I know for a fact you ain't stupid. What was the idea of sending the men away and leavin' us without horses?'

'I got horses.' came the even reply. 'At least I got two horses,' Lauren Wex said, coming from behind the corner of the house and advancing on the pair behind a cocked sawn-off shotgun.

'I also know about the old man's book,' she went on, addressing Rosa, while motioning Owen to stillness with an imperious jerk of the weapon's barrel. 'I've known about it for years and I figure you an' me'd make a good team.'

'I'm admittin' that we probably would, except I ain't got the book,' Rosa admitted.

'Oh, and why might that be?' the other demanded, although her self-satisfied smirk showed plainly that she had most of the answers before she asked the questions.

'Because my ever-lovin' born stupid brother Stark took the damn thing to town the day he got shot, and now I don't know where the hell it is!' Rosa snapped, irritated at having to admit to what she considered her own failure.

'Where would you guess it might be then?' Lauren Wex asked silkily.

'I'm guessin' that damn marshal's probably got it. From what I hear, he ain't one to miss any bets!' she snarled, glaring at her little brother, who seemed to shrink under the blazing scrutiny.

'Well, a couple of hours ago, that would have been a perfect guess,' the other conceded with a low laugh, 'but, you see, after I knifed the fat Mexican bitch they left guarding me, I went through the marshal's desk. And I not only found the book but all the papers he took from the ship. He had the whole organization laid out,' she finished, 'but now I've got it!'

'So he's got no evidence,' Rosa exclaimed triumphantly.

'Exactly,' the other agreed, 'and with the boys dead, what's to stop you claiming you were an innocent party the whole time? You inherit the ranch, free and clear.' she went on. 'I've got the book and the other stuff. Once things have cooled down, we can start again.'

'Sounds perfect,' Rosa admitted. 'Only one other thing: what about him?' she went on, jerking a thumb at a livid Owen Ducane, held powerless while these two despised females decided his fate.

'Oh little Owen has always been

useless baggage,' Lauren Wex began sweetly, raising the sawn-off, 'so I guess we won't be needing him. That is' — she paused — 'unless you have any strenuous objections?'

'Like Pa said once, the little bastard ain't never been worth the food he ate. Two can sure travel lighter than three,' Rosa finished callously.

'Now, just hold on a goddamn minute,' Owen snarled, although the snarl was at least half whine, 'you're gonna need me!'

'What for?' Lauren Wex demanded with a shrug, as she lifted her weapon, finger tightening on the trigger.

Screwing his eyes shut, Owen Ducane tried to brace himself for the shock of the buckshot. It didn't come, however, because before the woman could exert the last ounce of pressure on the trigger, there came a stentorian bellow from the nearby livery barn.

'This is Deputy Federal Marshal Fargo Reilly! Throw down your guns! You're all under arrest!'

17

'Christ,' Owen Ducane whined, as the trio retreated into the house, 'how in hell did he get here so goddamn quick with a posse?'

'How in hell would I know?' Rosa snarled in vicious mimicry. 'What we gotta worry about now is how we're gonna get rid of him. Any bright ideas?' she snapped, glaring across at her prospective partner.

'Perhaps,' came the cool reply. 'Get me a white cloth and don't waste any time.'

★   ★   ★

Of all the responses Reilly could have foreseen, the white flag he saw waving from the second-storey window, was probably the one he least expected.

Cautiously remaining in cover, he awaited developments, which, as it turned out, were not long in coming.

'*Marshal!*' Rosa Ducane bellowed from the main door. 'We're quittin'. Owen's wounded pretty bad and I got no gun! You better get up here if you wanna see Owen hang! He's liable to bleed to death, if he ain't fixed up.'

'Come out on the porch where I can see you,' Reilly retorted, smoothly drawing both his Colts, having made sure that the big Le Mat was at least partially concealed by his long-backed calfskin vest.

'Try any tricks and you'll both die quick!' he gritted.

'Back up,' Reilly ordered, having reached the house and cautiously mounted the porch steps. Rosa Ducane moved back into the house, hands held loosely at shoulder height.

'Just like I said, Marshal,' she said, indicating her apparently unconscious brother, prone on the floor, as she moved back to stand over him, 'you better do something quick, or he'll up and die on you!'

'Step away from him,' Reilly began, lowering his guns and advancing sideways into the house so as to leave the open door to his right. 'He don't look — '

'Drop your guns, Marshal!' Lauren Wex snapped, pushing back the main door, behind which she had been hiding, and levelling the wicked-looking shot-gun. 'Even I couldn't miss at this range!'

'I guess you couldn't at that,' Reilly admitted, carefully placing his weapons on the floor before straightening up and pushing both hands into the back strap of his jeans, his right hand almost touching the angular butt of the big Le Mat.

'Well, now,' Rosa Ducane snarled, moving to stand within reach of the man from Tucson, 'I guess you ain't so high and mighty now, Mr Federal Marshal, are you?'

'You tell me,' Reilly replied mildly, 'seems like you're holding most o' the cards.'

'Damn right we are!' Owen Ducane yelled in turn, rising and moving to stand between Reilly and Lauren Wex while lifting his hand to hover over the butt of his single remaining Colt.

'An' now, if you wanna live, all you gotta do is reach down and pick up one o' them guns before I use mine,' Ducane snarled. 'Go ahead, Mr Gunfighter, make your play!'

'You goin' along with this?' Reilly demanded nervously, bringing his left hand from his belt to point directly at Rosa Ducane and, in doing so, drawing every eye away from his right, now grasping the butt of his remaining pistol.

'Hell, Marshal. I guess you're just gonna have to do the best you can,' the woman sneered, backing away slightly to leave space between her brother and his intended victim.

'OK,' Reilly shrugged, the lifting of his right shoulder being followed instantly by the appearance of the Le Mat, the big pistol kicking in his hand as he triggered a shot at Owen Ducane.

Caught in the left shoulder by the heavy .44 bullet, Owen was driven backwards towards the main door, his gun still holstered, as Reilly thumb-cocked the heavy revolver, dropping flat and swinging his weapon towards Lauren Wex.

Desperately jerking up the heavy sawn-off, Reilly's second shot caught her in the chest and, triggered with her dying reflex, both barrels of her gun exploded, sending their charge into the wall next to Rosa Ducane, who was in the act of drawing her tiny derringer.

Shaken by the spray of closely passing pellets, she hesitated, trying to line her weapon on Reilly, who in the split second allowed him, snapped two shots into Rosa Ducane's chest an instant before her finger could tighten on the trigger.

Terror-stricken by the speed with which Reilly had dealt with the two women and without a glance at his badly injured or dying sister, Ducane stumbled through the main door into the blinding noonday sunlight. Apparently without thinking, he veered across the front of the house, heading at a stumbling run towards the mesquite patch.

★ ★ ★

'Looks like you still beat us,' Rosa Ducane managed weakly, as Reilly knelt beside her and began to make a rapid survey of her wounds.

'Lie still,' he ordered. 'I'll get you to town and — '

'Don't be a fool,' the woman snapped, without heat. 'I ain't gonna last ten minutes and we both know it. How many you bring in that posse?'

'I came alone,' Reilly admitted, 'but Miz Ducane, if you can speak, there's somethin' I gotta know. It's about Miz Wex's boy,' Reilly went on. 'Where'd the old man send him to school?'

'There never was no boy,' Rosa gasped, managing a weak smile at the surprise on Reilly's face. 'Billy, her husband, was the eldest and worst of all of us,' she said. 'He was madder even than the old man, and believe me that's saying something.' She paused, mouthing weakly, to allow Reilly to wipe the blood from her lips and chin.

'Lauren was a whore workin' in some El Paso cat-house,' she went on. 'She turned up here with Billy's body and a marriage licence and the old man took her in. Pa and her were . . . well . . . I guess you can figure it . . . out,' she said, after a long pause, her voice barely rising to a painful whisper. 'But . . . she never had no children. Couldn't, on account . . . Billy givin' . . . her . . . syphilis. Gave it . . . to the ol' man . . . too. Guess . . . she . . . must have . . . been stone . . . mad . . . ' The girl's head slumped on to her chest and Reilly laid the limp body carefully on the floor.

'Guess she musta been at that,' he admitted softly.

Looking up, his face set like flint.

'So that just leaves one,' he informed himself softly, shoving cartridges into the Le Mat's empty chambers, before reaching down to retrieve his Colts.

★ ★ ★

The wound in Owen Ducane's shoulder had ceased to bleed, but it had now begun to throb with an agonizing intensity which made it hard to think.

Seated with his back to a twisted mesquite trunk deep in a large thicket well away from the edge of the patch, Ducane began belatedly to consider his options.

First on the list had to be dealing with that damn marshal, although that looked like being a job too dangerous for Ducane's liking. Far better, if he could manage it, to get away and leave revenge until a safer opportunity presented itself.

Escape, however, meant a horse and that meant going back to the house, where Reilly would be waiting.

'Ducane!' a hard voice bellowed from some distance. Still not in the mesquite, a tiny voice trilled in Ducane's mind. Perhaps there was a chance after all.

'What d'you want, damn it?' Ducane called weakly. 'I'm hit bad, in the lungs, I think,' he lied. 'I'm a dead man, Marshal, and, like Rosa said, you better help me if you want to see me hang.'

Swiftly, Ducane pushed his last two cartridges into his pistol, before scrabbling around so that his right hand, now clutching his remaining Colt, was hidden from view.

He had barely finished his preparations when he heard a single scuffling footfall and Reilly appeared through a break in the surrounding brush.

'Thank God,' Ducane mumbled, feigning delirium. 'Help . . . me . . . for God's sake . . . help me.'

For a moment, Reilly glared bleakly down at this, the last of the band he had sworn to kill, then, with a grimace at his own weakness, he holstered his Colt and bent to examine his victim's wound. This was all Ducane had been waiting for.

With a scream of triumph, the wounded man swept up his pistol and fired. But the scream had given Reilly just enough warning, so, as the weapon appeared from behind Ducane's back, Reilly thrust himself away, knocking the pistol sideways, so the bullet tore a long bloody furrow in his thigh instead of blowing a hole in his stomach or chest as the shooter intended.

Dazed by the shock of his wound and momentarily stunned by his fall, Reilly could only watch as Ducane rose shakily to his knees and lifted the pistol.

'I'm sure gonna enjoy this,' Owen began, when there was a rustle from the bushes by Reilly's left shoulder.

Ducane paused, looking up, and what he saw there caused the pistol to drop from his limp, shaking hand.

'No . . . no . . . ' he screamed, incoherent with terror. 'No . . . it can't be . . . you can't be here . . . you were dead . . . hanging from the post . . . No one could have lived after what I . . . we did to you!'

Forgetful of his enemy, forgetful of his pistol, forgetful of everything except his need to escape, Ducane turned and plunged through the brush away from whatever it was that had inspired his terror.

★ ★ ★

'I sure as hell don't know what's got into him,' Reilly told himself when, having tied up his leg and found that he could still walk on it, after a fashion, he had examined the brush behind him, intent on finding who or what had driven Owen Ducane to near insanity.

Of the who or what, however, Reilly found not a trace. Not a sign or track; in fact, not even a trace of a trace and it was with his neck hairs twitching, that Reilly left the scene of what had so nearly been his own death and began following Owen Ducane through the close growing brush, to determine whatever the man's fate might have been.

It wasn't long before the man from Tucson found his erstwhile victim.

Ducane had caught his foot in one of the innumerable tough twisted roots which mesquite produces in such abundance, and fallen full length, to land on a pointed stake, the remains of a thick trunk, which had entered his chest, piercing his lung and exiting from his back.

He might have still been breathing but Reilly knew he was looking at a dead man. He bent, stretching to feel a pulse and Ducane's eyelids flickered upwards, terrified eyes starting out of his pale, bloodstained face.

'Don't let . . . him . . . get me . . . ' Ducane gasped brokenly, gripping Reilly's arm with a strength born of desperation. 'Don't . . . let him . . . '

'All right, it's all right,' Reilly soothed, moved almost to pity for his terrified victim.

'He come through the brush . . . '

Ducane went on, breath coming in strangled gasps and the froth bloody on his lips. 'I seen him . . . I . . . '

'Who?' Reilly demanded.

'The Indian . . . ' Ducane panted, 'Apache . . . kid . . . you . . . ' Then his body heaved convulsively and Owen Ducane was gone.

★ ★ ★

It was several hours later that a weary Pecos paced up Perdition's main street and stopped at the worn hitching rail before the marshal's office, allowing Reilly to fall ungracefully from the saddle into the dirt of the street.

'Better get out to the Ducane place, Matt,' Reilly slurred, as Crane lifted him carefully from the dirt. 'Gotta bury what's left o' them, afore the buzzards get their share.

'Find Mangas, too,' he finished. 'The boy'll . . . mebbe rest . . . easier . . . now.'

And, with his duty done, the Marshal of Perdition promptly fainted again.

18

'I ain't just sure *what* he saw,' Reilly admitted uneasily, shifting his injured leg, in an attempt to find a place where Crane's abundant bandaging didn't rub.

'He was sure convinced, though. What you gonna put in your report, *Marshal*?' he went on, placing clear emphasis on the last word, and grinning down at the badge pinned to Crane's worn vest.

'I'm writin' that you shot the li'l bastard in the back,' Crane snapped irascibly.

Laboriously he wrote another word before looking up and saying, 'Seriously, Fargo, I still ain't got the whole business straight yet. You say Miz Wex, or Ducane, or whatever you call her, was married to one o' the Ducanes?'

'That's one of a few things I ain't

sure about,' Reilly admitted, 'but as near as I can figure it, Miz Wex come down here from El Paso with a marriage certificate, claimin' to be Billy Ducane's wife.

'From what you tell me,' he went on, 'the gun-runnin' started about the time she arrived, so I'm guessin', mebbe it was her idea.

'Anyhow, they built the barns, found the caves and laid out their routes over the border, through a coupla l'il towns like Dragon Wells that didn't pay much attention to strangers passin' through as long as they paid well.'

'Why'd they need to stop in towns at all?' Crane asked.

'I think they was usin' them as collection points,' Reilly suggested. 'Anyhow,' he went on, 'things was going swell, when ol' man Ducane gets ideas above his station and starts meddlin' in Mex politics. That an' Buck Ducane gettin' a hankerin' for someone else's gal was all it took.'

'He didn't burn Dragon Wells 'cause

they killed Buck,' Reilly finished in explanation. 'He burnt the town 'cause he couldn't take a chance that someone had seen them Gatlin's. More importantly, he couldn't take a chance someone had seen the boxes they was in.'

'The boxes,' Crane said wonderingly. 'What was so important about the boxes?'

Grunting with pain, Reilly reached down next to his chair and lifted a substantial piece of timber on to his lap.

It was in reality two boards, cleated together with two substantial battens and, with what had been the outer surface of the crate turned towards him, Crane could clearly make out a series of letters, even though a half-hearted attempt had been made to plane them off.

'S.P.R.I.N.G.F. — can't see the rest. Then it looks like A.R.M . . . ' Crane read slowly, before realization suddenly dawned.

'Goddamit, Fargo!' he snapped, It

says Springfield Armoury! You mean the old bastard was stealin' government guns?'

'Looks like it,' Reilly admitted, 'He an' Miz Wex musta had one hell of an organization.'

'Christ, you're telling me!' came the old man's vehement reply. 'What put you on to them?'

'It was them wide tyres that started me thinkin',' Reilly admitted. 'They had to be haulin' somethin' heavy across a bad surface. Soon as I saw the bay here, I started to put two and two together. Also Miz Wex's barn was the only one they could use without comin' through town.

'Guess there'll be some pokin' around up north as well as in Mexico City, afore this here business is cleared up,' Reilly finished.

★ ★ ★

'Sure wish you could stick around a while longer, Fargo.' Crane admitted gruffly, squinting up at his friend sitting easily in the saddle of an impatient Pecos, some days later.

'Naw you don't, Matt.' Reilly grinned easily. 'My job's done here and *hombres* like me, well, they make decent folks uneasy.

'I'll be seeing you, Matt,' Reilly went on, twitching Pecos's reins and turning away from the hitching rail.

'*Adios . . . amigo*,' Crane said softly, watching the tall, spare figure, disappearing into the strong south-western sunlight.

THE END

WOLVERHAMPTON
LIBRARIES

We do hope that you have enjoyed
reading this large print book.

Did you know that all of our titles
are available for purchase?

We publish a wide range of high
quality large print books including:
Romances, Mysteries, Classics
General Fiction
Non Fiction and Westerns

Special interest titles available in
large print are:
The Little Oxford Dictionary
Music Book, Song Book
Hymn Book, Service Book

Also available from us courtesy of
Oxford University Press:
Young Readers' Dictionary
(large print edition)
Young Readers' Thesaurus
(large print edition)

For further information or a free
brochure, please contact us at:
Ulverscroft Large Print Books Ltd.,
The Green, Bradgate Road, Anstey,
Leicester, LE7 7FU, England.
Tel: (00 44) **0116 236 4325**
Fax: (00 44) **0116 234 0205**

BOTH SIDES OF THE LAW

Hank J. Kirby

A full hand in draw poker changed Hardin's life — and almost ended it. First there was the shoot-out with the house gambler. Then suspicion of bank robbery, enforced recruitment into a posse, gunfights in the hills and pursuit by both sides of the law in strange country. He'd never had so much trouble! What should he do? Drift on, away from this hellhole, or stay and fight? There was no real choice — it was fight or die . . .

LIZARD WELLS

Caleb Rand

After losing his whole family to a bloodthirsty army patrol, Ben Brooke takes to the desolate Ozark snowline. Years later, he returns to the town called Lizard Wells, where the guilty soldiers have degenerated into guerrillas, bringing brutal disorder to the town. Also living there is the tough Erma Flagg — and more importantly, Moses, a young Cheyenne half-breed . . . After a wild thunderstorm crushes the town, Ben, in desperate need of help, chooses to step single-handedly into a final reckoning.

MISFIT LIL FIGHTS BACK

Chap O'Keefe

Misfit Lil wouldn't allow the rustlers to run off some of her pa's improved Flying G beeves. She started a stampede that trampled them bloodily into the dust. But then two assassins gunned down horse rancher Sundown Sander's son Jimmie. And he had made no move to defend himself, despite Lil's stormy ride to bring him warning. Could devious madam Kitty Malone or gambling-hall owner Flash Sam Whittaker tell the truth about Jimmie's fatal resignation? Lil had to find out.

SHOOT-OUT AT BIG KING

Lee Lejeune

Billy Bandro arrives in Freshwater
Creek in Wyoming to start a new life
away from riding with the killer
outlaw Wesley Toms. When Toms is
captured, Billy is assigned to drive
him to Laramie for trial, but Toms'
gang bushwhack the coach, leave Billy
for dead, and take Nancy Partridge
and her Aunt Emily hostage. The
gambler Slam Beardsley saves Billy,
and they ride off in pursuit. But there
are many surprises for them in the
mountains . . .